"I want you to rub the oil lightly across the tops of your shoulders and in random spots on your chest and back," Alice told Lance.

"How random?" His teeth flashed whitely in his bronzed face as he grinned wickedly at her. He couldn't remember when he'd had such fun with a woman. Alice was shy and prim in an old-fashioned way, yet she could have turned Sherman back from the burning of Atlanta and made him smile while retreating.

Alice considered Lance's question, and her face flushed. Her hands fluttered vaguely in the air. "Oh, just here and there."

"I'm afraid you'll have to show me, ma'am," he drawled with some pleasure. "Besides, I can't reach my back."

She had to stop and consider if she was still breathing. Telling herself she was a grown woman and could handle this, she walked up to his broad golden back as if it were a rope and she were about to be hanged. He was just an ordinary man, just muscle and bone, she reminded herself. So why were her knees buckling?

She lifted one hand and hesitantly smoothed oil across his upper back. The first contact with Lance's smoothly muscled body sent a shock wave that nearly knocked her off her feet. . .

WHAT ARE *LOVESWEPT* ROMANCES?

They are stories of true romance and touching emotion. We
believe those two very important ingredients are constants
in our highly sensual and very believable stories in the
LOVESWEPT line. Our goal is to give you, the reader,
stories of consistently high quality that may sometimes make
you laugh, sometimes make you cry, but are always fresh
and creative and contain many delightful surprises within
their pages.

Most romance fans read an enormous number of books.
Those they truly love, they keep. Others may be traded with
friends and soon forgotten. We hope that each *LOVESWEPT*
romance will be a treasure—a "keeper." We will always try
to publish

*LOVE STORIES YOU'LL NEVER FORGET
BY AUTHORS YOU'LL ALWAYS REMEMBER*

The Editors

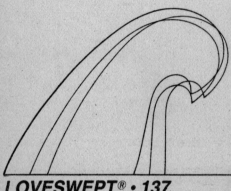

LOVESWEPT® • 137

Peggy Webb
Tarnished Armor

BANTAM BOOKS
TORONTO • NEW YORK • LONDON • SYDNEY • AUCKLAND

TARNISHED ARMOR

A Bantam Book / April 1986

ISBN 0-553-21750-X

Published simultaneously in the United States and Canada

Bantam Books are published by Bantam Books, Inc. Its
trademark, consisting of the words "Bantam Books" and
the portrayal of a rooster, is Registered in U.S. Patent and
Trademark Office and in other countries. Marca Registrada.
Bantam Books, Inc., 666 Fifth Avenue, New York, New
York 10103.

PRINTED IN THE UNITED STATES OF AMERICA

O   0 9 8 7 6 5 4 3 2 1

One

"What I need is a *real* man." Alice Spencer shoved her glasses up into her neatly coiled hair and glared at her secretary. "Just look at these." She riffled through the stack of eight-by-ten black-and-white glossies on her desk and let them drop, one by one, into the wastebasket. "He's too short." Plop! Into the wastebasket. "That one has too much hair. Just look at the self-satisfied smirk on this one's face. Heaven forbid I should be caught dead with this slick dude." She stood up and paced the gray carpet in front of her polished mahogany desk like a caged lioness. "Just tell me, Linda, where are all the real men?"

Linda pushed her fluff of red hair behind her ears and chewed thoughtfully on the end of her pencil before answering her boss. "Perhaps if you called Models Unlimited . . ."

"Bah!" Alice Spencer walked to her closet, took down her sensible felt hat, and rammed it on her head. "I don't want a cardboard man to advertise Eduardo's new line of clothes. I want somebody with guts and brawn and craggy lines and bulging muscles. I want a man who makes your mouth go dry just to look at him."

She flicked at a speck of dust on her perfectly tailored, sensible navy-blue wool suit, turned on her perfectly polished Italian leather shoes, and marched toward the door.

"Where are you going, Miss Spencer?" squeaked Linda as she regarded her boss with reverent awe. Alice Spencer was always doing things to make Linda squeak, unexpected things like using huge, vicious Doberman pinschers in her television ads when nice, docile Chihuahuas would do just as well. And climbing up mountains to get a good shot when a small, safe hill would suffice. And going out on water skis herself to direct an ad, although she couldn't even swim.

"I'm going out to find a man," Miss Alice Spencer said, and shut the door smartly behind her. Her mind whirled with all the efficiency of a computer as she walked to the elevator and pressed the down button. Where would she find a real man? she asked herself. A local bar? No, too sleazy. She needed a man with the healthy look of an outdoorsman. A seaman or a fisherman. That was it.

She nodded to herself with satisfaction as she stepped from the elevator in Government Center and walked out into the apple-crisp October day. The wind whipped her skirt around her shapely legs as she headed south on Congress Street and hailed a cab. "Boston Harbor, please," she told the cabdriver.

As the grand old buildings of downtown Boston whizzed by, Alice sat back in her seat and relaxed. It never occurred to her that she would not find the man she wanted, or that once she found him he would not be willing to do the job. She had run her own business for seven years and was accustomed to problems. Problems didn't defeat Alice—she defeated them.

The breeze threatened to whip her hat from her head as she left the taxi. She reached up and anchored her hatpin more securely, then marched confidently down the docks, scanning every boat anchored in the harbor. She rejected the yachts and concentrated on the sailboats. From a distance she saw two likely looking candidates, but as she moved closer she saw that they were too old.

She came to the end of the slips where the pleasure boats were moored. There was nothing else in the harbor except a ratty looking old lobster boat. Nothing there, of course. She wasn't looking for scruffy, just virile. Maybe she had missed something on the sailboats.

As she turned sharply, the wind lifted her sensible felt hat off her head, dislodging some of the pins in her hair, and capriciously sailed it toward the smelly lobster boat. Instinctively, she whirled back around and reached for the hat. With her hand in midair, she stopped. My Lord, she thought. There he was, just emerging from the hold of the lobster boat. His hair gleamed like freshly mown wheat and his teeth flashed whitely in his sun-bronzed, gorgeous face. Pure male-animal gorgeous. Virile. Dashing. A careless vagabond. He was everything she wanted him to be.

Her hat completely forgotten, Alice Spencer walked boldly to the edge of the dock and opened her mouth to hail her discovery. Her tongue clung to a dry roof, and she had to pull herself together before she could speak. "Excuse me!" she called, waving a hand to attract the man's attention. "I have a proposition for you." She said the words without blushing. When Alice had business to conduct she didn't pussyfoot around.

The man glanced in her direction, examined her from the top of her wind-ruffled hair to the tips of her leather shoes, lifted one perfect eyebrow, and turned his attention to the lobster trap in his hand.

Alice didn't take kindly to being ignored. She drew herself up to her full five feet seven and girded herself for battle. "I'm talking to you," she said in a no-nonsense voice.

The careless vagabond glanced back over his shoulder at her and lifted his eyebrow once more in a way that made Alice's mouth go dry—again. Damn! she thought. He was perfect. She couldn't wait to get him to Puerto Vallarta. She could see the swell of his muscles under his jersey as he swung the trap into a holding tank.

She had to have him. Maybe bribery would work. "I'll make it worth your while if you'll give me a few minutes of your time."

Lines of amusement crinkled his face as the dashing fisherman finally spoke to her. "You get right to the point, don't you? I never expected that from a proper Bostonian lady." He grinned hugely. "Where I come from," he drawled, "it takes more than a few minutes."

Alice Spencer didn't bat an eyelash. She was too intrigued by his speech. It rolled off his tongue like molasses and mint juleps. He was from the South, no doubt about it. The way his rs came out as ahs. Alice guessed one of the Carolinas. "I'm talking money, not dillydallying," she said. "Big money. Could you come down so I don't have to shout?"

The bronzed fisherman tucked his thumbs into

the belt loops of his blue jeans and stood firmly on the deck. "I'm not for sale."

"I don't want to buy you, just hire you," she snapped. He was beginning to get under her skin. Careful, she told herself. You have to stay in control of the situation.

"I'm not interested."

"How do you know? You haven't even heard what the job is."

"I don't want to hear what the job is." He turned his back to her and started to walk away.

"Wait!" she shouted. She mustn't let him get away. "I can take you away from all this." She waved her arm to encompass the decrepit lobster boat and the blue waters of the bay.

The blond fisherman slowly turned back around. "I don't believe I've ever met such a pushy woman. You might as well come on board and tell me where you propose to take me and what you plan to do with me when we get there. I haven't had a good laugh all day long. Besides"—he leaned over the lobster tank and retrieved a soggy mass of felt— "you have to get your hat."

Alice looked at her ruined hat—it was a small price to pay for finding this man—then at the hulk before her, riding low in the water. "How do I get on board?"

"I'll lower the gangplank, but you have to watch your step."

When she saw the rickety board he lowered to the pier she had her first doubts about the success of her venture. What if she fell through that damn board into the bay? She couldn't even swim. On the other hand, he'd have to fish her out. Alice pushed her glasses securely onto her nose and stepped confidently onto the gangplank. The fisherman leaned casually on the boat rail and watched her progress.

She was almost to the top when her sharp heel sank through a rotten place in the board. Alice teetered uncertainly for a moment, flailing her arms in the air to regain her balance. Her glasses fell to the end of her nose and the rest of the pins flew from her hair. Impatiently, she jerked her foot upward, freeing the stuck shoe and catapulting herself onto the deck of the lobster boat.

She brushed her heavy hair out of her face, pushed her glasses back up on her nose, and glared at the grinning fisherman. "I thought all Southern men were gallant toward ladies."

"You've been reading the wrong books. Besides, ladies don't proposition men." He boldly assessed his visitor and decided that, up close, she wasn't bad looking for somebody dressed in such stuffy clothes. She had guts, too, walking that gangplank the way she had. He admired a woman with spirit.

"It's just a damn good thing I didn't fall into the bay," she said tartly.

"Ladies don't cuss either." he drawled. His eyes crinkled with amusement.

"Forget about ladies," she snapped. "I'm not here to discuss decorum. I'm here to do business."

"Not to 'dillydally'?" he teased. He was loving every minute of this unusual situation. He was tempted to take her into his arms just to see her reaction. Damned if she didn't have more spunk than a jaybird at a wren party.

"Of course not," Alice said. "I don't dillydally." She knew she was fast losing control of the situation. And besides that, this man was making her mouth dry again, just standing there with the sunshine glinting in his wheat-colored hair and that absolutely marvelous smile on his face.

"I thought not," he said, once again looking her over from head to toe.

The unflappable Alice Spencer blushed. Falling into the bay suddenly seemed a desirable alternative to talking with this brazen fisherman. She glanced up at the sky, where a lone sea gull was wheeling by. She wasn't accustomed to having to pull herself together. "I'm Alice Spencer," she said when the blood stopped pounding in her ears, "owner of Spencer Productions. I'm looking for a man—"

"You are?"

"To use—"

"How outrageous of you!"

"In my television commercials." She let out a small puff of breath in relief. Good Lord, was he worth it?

"How disappointing. And all this time I thought you wanted to dillydally." Even when he tried to look crestfallen he was still ruinously gorgeous.

Alice plunged boldly on, choosing to ignore both his outrageous remarks and his outrageous behavior. "Eduardo Velasquez has designed a line of clothes for men, and I have been searching for the right man to use in the television commercials that I'll be producing and directing." The wind kept whipping her hair into her face, and she kept reaching up to push it back. She realized she wasn't dressed for being on a lobster boat in Massachusetts Bay on a windy October day. Each movement of her arm worked her silk blouse loose from her skirt's waistband. She finally pushed her glasses to the top of her head to anchor her hair, but she refused to tuck her blouse inside her skirt in front of a man. This man, in particular.

"You are the right man . . ." she went on.

"How gratifying."

He was doing it again, she thought. She was tempted to turn on her heel and tell Eduardo to find somebody else to film the commercials. Almost, but not quite. Alice Spencer was no quitter. "I'm prepared to offer you a fabulous contract that will pay you to travel to exotic places and will even pay you to become famous. TV fans all over America will recognize you as the man in the El Hombre ads."

"El Hombre?" His voice held a spark of interest.

"That's the name of Eduardo's line of clothes."

" 'The Man,' " he said musingly. "Interesting." For the past two weeks he had been feeling the familiar restlessness that told him it was time to move on. With a suddenness that was characteristic of him, he mentally detached himself from the lobster boat and plunged, full speed ahead, into this new venture.

"How soon does this job start?" he asked. The decision made, he was eager for the change. From somewhere deep inside him a small hope rose, a hope almost buried under layers of indifference cultivated by his vagabond lifestyle. Maybe this time he would find what he was looking for, that elusive something that would burrow under his skin, next to his heart, and give him a reason to stop searching, a reason to put down roots.

Alice felt like clicking her heels in glee, but she suppressed the urge. Instead, she smiled brightly at him. "We can have lunch with Eduardo tomorrow, and if he approves—and I'm sure he will—we'll be leaving next week for Puerto Vallarta."

"And how long will the job last?"

"If everything goes as planned, we'll be finished by Christmas. We'll go south first to film the ads for the spring and summer lines. After that we'll travel back north while the leaves are still colorful to film next fall's line. Between Thanksgiving and Christmas we'll go on location—probably in Colorado—to do next winter's line. That's only the beginning, of course. Periodically we'll be getting together to film new commercials for Eduardo. The opportunities are unlimited."

He grinned a wicked grin. "I like the sound of that."

Somehow, Alice thought of dillydallying again. She pulled her mind quickly away from the thought. She was anxious to lock up the deal and get off this lobster boat. "Will twelve-thirty tomorrow at Locke-Ober be satisfactory? Or would you prefer a restaurant that's a little less formal?"

"I'll muddle through somehow, Miss Spencer." The obsequious manner rang false, but Alice couldn't quite put her finger on why.

She turned to leave, and the twisting motion released the rest of her blouse from her waistband. A devilish puff of wind whipped the delicate fabric sharply, causing the top button of her blouse to gap open. Alice didn't dare turn back around, so she said over her shoulder, "By the way, what is your name?"

"Today, I call myself Lance, short for Lancelot." He moved forward swiftly and put his arms around her from behind. "And by the way, Alice, your blouse is untucked." With deft motions, he tucked her silk blouse back into her skirt.

Alice nearly had a heart attack. She stood so still

it was hard to tell whether or not she was breathing. When he released her she nearly fell.

"See you tomorrow, Alice."

She was in no condition to reply. She left the lobster boat and walked down the gangplank in a fog. Providence guided her around the rotten places in the board, for her legs were marshmallows and her brain had ceased to function.

She didn't remember calling a taxi or directing him to Government Center, but she must have, for now she stood outside her office building, still clutching the front of her blouse. Her fingers released the fabric as if it were hot. What if he had seen that the front of her blouse was open? Would he have fixed that too? As she walked shakily inside to the elevator she shivered, thinking of those long, bronze fingers buttoning the top of her blouse. She covered her blouse front with her hands as if to shield herself from such an unsettling intrusion.

When the elevator doors slid open with electronic efficiency on the tenth floor, instinct guided Alice down the hall to Room 1002. Automatically, she walked to her closet and reached to the top of her head to remove her hat. She stood for a second with a handful of empty air, then remembered that she had lost her hat. Slowly she glided over to her desk and sat down.

The door to Linda's office cracked open and Linda's tousled red head appeared around the corner. "Is that you, Miss Spencer?" Receiving no reply, she stepped into her boss's office, steno pad and pencil in hand. If Miss Spencer had found her man, Linda knew she would be ready to snap out orders like a drill sergeant.

Halfway into the office, Linda stopped and gazed

at her boss in amazement. Miss Spencer's hair was tumbled about her shoulders, held rakishly in place by the glasses on top of her head. The top button of her blouse was open, and the blouse appeared to be tucked into her skirt crookedly. Linda had never seen her boss like that before. "Miss Spencer?" she asked tentatively.

Alice focused her eyes on the object in the center of her office. The object was speaking to her. Good Lord, it was Linda. She grabbed her glasses off the top of her head and settled them firmly on her nose. "Yes, Linda?" Her voice, she noticed bemusedly, had lost some of its snap.

"Did you find him?"

"Who?"

"The man you were looking for?"

"The man?" Alice shook her head to clear it. "Oh, yes. The man. I found him all right." She reached up and patted her hair absently.

"Well?"

Linda was speaking in riddles, Alice thought. She didn't often get annoyed with her secretary, but Linda was trying her patience right now. "Linda, will you please speak in complete sentences?" Some of the starch was beginning to come back into Alice's voice.

"I'm dying to know what he looks like and who he is." Linda sat down on the Queen Anne chair facing her boss's desk and leaned forward eagerly.

"Well, he's . . ." Alice's voice trailed off and her eyes became unfocused. She was sure the front of her blouse was heaving up and down with the furious pumping of her heart. She adjusted her glasses to steady herself. "He's tall and blond. Very good-looking. A bronzed outdoorsman. He's a lobster fisherman."

Linda inched forward on her seat. "You went all the way to the harbor?" she squeaked.

"Yes. The wind played havoc with my hair while I was there." And the lobster fisherman played havoc with her mind, she finished to herself.

"A lobster fisherman!" Linda clapped her hands in delight. "He sound perfect. I can just see him in Eduardo's swim trunks."

Alice swallowed convulsively. She could too. And that was the trouble. "His name is Lancelot, Linda."

"Lancelot? Like the knights of the Round Table?"

"That's what he said. He's obviously a drifter. He probably takes a new name with every new job."

"He sounds romantic to me."

Linda was almost off her seat, Alice thought. If she scooted forward half an inch more, she'd be on the floor. Alice took a deep breath and noted with relief that her pulse had slowed to almost normal and the blood was flowing back to her brain. "We'll wait until tomorrow afternoon to draw up his contract, Linda. There's a small possibility that Eduardo won't approve him."

"I can't imagine why. He sounds like a dreamboat to me, Miss Spencer."

Alice's laugh sounded shaky even to herself. "What we need is a model, not a dreamboat."

Linda rose from her seat. "Everybody needs a dreamboat." She cocked her head to one side and chewed on the end of her pencil as she studied her boss. "Do you need me for dictation or anything?"

"No." Alice glanced at the clock on her desk. It was four o'clock. "You can go home early today. I need to leave early myself to make arrangements for Mark."

After Linda left Alice walked to her bathroom to make repairs on her hair. With quick, efficient motions, she brushed her hair and pinned it into a neat coil. Her flushed face looked back at her from the mirror. She smoothed her skirt around her hips and reached inside the waistband to straighten her blouse, then froze. She could feel again his large hands smoothing the silk blouse against her silk slip. With his hands on her skin, a slow heat had spread throughout her body. Alice stood in her bathroom, mortified. What bothered her most was that she had liked it.

Two

Alice almost never drove her car anywhere except to work because she hated driving through the congested city streets. But she loved Beacon Hill. The cool, tree-lined streets, the gas street lamps, the brick sidewalks, and the eighteenth- and nineteenth-century houses made driving there a pleasure. Her own nineteenth-century house at 33 Mt. Vernon was across the street from the one-time home of Julia Ward Howe. To Alice, coming home was like stepping backward into the pages of history.

She parked her car in the garage behind her house and walked through the back door into her brick-floored kitchen. Her nephew plummeted around the corner and into her arms.

"Guess what, Aunt Alice! We did our times tables at school today and I was the only one in class who did the sevens!"

"That's fantastic, Mark. I think that deserves a special hug." She squeezed her eight-year-old nephew.

Mrs. Billingsley came in from the pantry with a steaming hot apple pie. "I know a better way to celebrate. Who would like a piece of apple pie?" She set the pie on the kitchen table, wiped her hands on her immaculate white apron, and winked at Mark.

"Before dinner, Mrs. B?" Alice asked in mind reproof.

"If we waited until after, it wouldn't be a celebration. It would just be dessert." With all the authority of one who is in complete charge in the home, Mrs. B set three plates on the table and cut three generous pieces of her delicious pie. "You might even find some ice cream in the freezer if you look real hard, Alice."

Alice obeyed Mrs. B without question. Seven years ago, when her sister had been killed and she had found herself with a year-old nephew to raise, Alice had had the good fortune to find Mrs. Billingsley. Mrs. B was a widow. Her grown children were dispersed to the far corners of the United States and she was lonely. Alice thought the agency that matched them deserved a medal. It was a match made in heaven. Mrs. B loved children, she loved to cook, and she loved Alice's house. Both Alice and Mark flourished under her loving attentions.

After their slices of the celebration pie had been eaten and more exciting pursuits had called Mark away, Alice sat at the table, talking with her housekeeper, friend, and surrogate mother. "I'm going on location next week to Puerto Vallarta," she said. "I thought I would take you and Mark with me."

Mrs. Billingsley nodded approvingly. "What will the school principal say?" she asked, her blue eyes twinkling.

"Probably the same thing he said when I took Mark out of school last spring to go to Spain. 'Miss Spencer, I think it would be more beneficial to Mark to leave him in school.' He's too dull to know that travel is the best education in the world."

Mrs. B chuckled as she rose from the table and began preparing a large pot roast for the oven. "He's no match for you," she said, smiling indulgently. "Tell me, what are you filming this time?"

"Commercials for Eduardo's new line of men's clothes." Alice's palms dampened as she thought of her model.

Mrs. B's eyes narrowed as she looked up at Alice. "Is the model handsome?"

"Now, Mrs. B, don't start that."

"What?" Mrs. B was the picture of innocence.

"Matchmaking."

"It's about time you stopped concentrating on Mark and your business and started thinking of yourself." Mrs. B shook pepper vigorously over her pot roast. "What you need is a man in your life."

"I have plenty of men in my life. There's Ralph." A mental picture of the quiet, unobtrusive sales representative came into her mind. She couldn't help but contrast him with the lobster fisherman. "When he's in town we go out together."

"Humph! I'll bet that's all you do."

Alice thought of Ralph's meek kisses and the ho-hum way she felt in his presence. She had never felt quivery and flushed in the presence of a man . . . until today. The heat rose in her face as she remembered the fisherman's hands on her skin. To cover her confusion she jumped up and began to putter about the kitchen, aimlessly picking up a jelly jar and moving it from one shelf to another. "Ralph's a nice man, a good man," she said.

"Has Ralph ever tried to put the make on you?" Mrs. B's knife snicked sharply against the cutting board as she sliced carrots for the pot roast.

The jelly jar slipped from Alice's hand and banged against the shelf. " 'Put the make on me'? Good grief, where did you pick up that expression?" Of course Ralph didn't try to maneuver her into his bed, she thought. He was too polite for that sort of thing. And that was perfectly fine with her. She didn't like complicated relationships.

"I thought not." Mrs. B dumped the carrots into the pot and stood with her hands on her hips, looking at Alice.

Mrs. B was the only person in the world who could make Alice squirm. "Making out, as you so indelicately put it, is for high school and college kids." She touched the cookie jar before returning to her chair at the table. "What is this anyhow, twenty questions?"

"Honey, I worry about you. You've had too much responsibility and too little time for fun. Not many girls of twenty-three have to take on raising a year-old baby and try to make a living, too. You've had seven years with your nose to the grindstone. I just think it's time you branched out."

The corners of Alice's mouth tipped up in a rueful smile. "While I was making a living the good ones got away." She glanced down at her folded hands, then back at Mrs. B. "But I have no regrets. I have a wonderful life, probably better than I would have had with a man. Look what happened to Heather."

"Your sister was a beautiful scatterbrain who made a bad match. Not all men abandon pregnant wives. Look at my Hugh. God never made a better man."

"You just got lucky. How can you tell which are the good men and which are the bad ones? Heather never could."

"You're not Heather." Mrs. B pursed her lips.

Alice ignored Mrs. B as she remembered the agony caused by Heather's poor choice of men. "After Marcus left Heather she got involved with a whole string of men. All louses. If it hadn't been for that last one, drunk on a sailboat, she would be alive today and Mark would have a mother."

"Mark has two mothers—you and me. What he needs is a father. Somebody to play ball with him in the backyard and teach him how to bait a fish-hook." Mrs. B banged the oven door shut for emphasis.

"That's what Little League is for," Alice snapped. Periodically, she and Mrs. B had this same discussion. They both knew the whole thing by heart. The snapping and banging was a part of the on-going argument and had nothing in the world to do with anger. "Besides, there are many father-less boys in our society, and they get by just fine with the loving support of one parent."

"And what about you? Is there a Little League for lonely career women?" Mrs. B punched down her bread dough and slapped it onto the breadboard with unusual vigor. Flour rose in small swirls as she kneaded the dough.

Little League for lonely career women? Alice repeated silently. This was a new play and she didn't know the script. "I'm not lonely. I have my career and my nephew."

"Just look at you." Mrs. B pointed a half-formed roll at Alice. "You're a beautiful woman, and it's all going to waste."

"Heather was the beauty, not me."

Mrs. B continued as if she hadn't heard Alice's protest. "Mark and I are the only ones who ever see the soft, lovely side of you. You put up a stern front, but I know better. Because of Heather's antics and her mistakes you've buried all your nesting instincts, but I have eyes. Somewhere inside you is a romantic woman longing for the right man to come along."

"You'd better have your eyes tested." Mrs. B was way off base, Alice told herself. She hadn't squelched anything. She had just been smart enough not to follow in her older sister's footsteps. Heather had never had any sense about men, and they had destroyed her. Alice knew better. "Nesting instincts? What have you been reading now?"

Mrs. B had recently embarked upon a self-improvement course that included reading every-thing that she thought would "broaden her horizons," a term she had picked up in *New Woman* and was fond of using. "Dr. Seuss," Mrs. B announced grandly as she buttered the tops of her rolls. She stopped, brush in midair, and cocked her gray head to one side. "Or maybe it was Dr. Spock. Anyhow, it was doctor somebody." She put the brush down and narrowed her eyes at Alice. "I'm not through on this subject yet, Alice. You need—"

"Aunt Alice!" Mark burst through the kitchen door, holding the pieces of a broken miniature car in his hand. "Can you fix it?"

Alice took her small nephew by the hand and led him from the kitchen, but not before she had seen Mrs. B's I-told-you-so look. "We'll repair it together," she said to Mark.

*   *   *

As Alice leaned in close to apply her mascara, her abundant brown hair fell in soft waves about her face. She lifted it with one hand. What if she left it loose? she wondered. She stood back and smoothed her jade wool suit over her hips. Not bad for thirty. With her hair swinging loose, she reached for her hat, and her gaze fell on Heather's picture. Beautiful Heather, with the periwinkle blue eyes and the silken blond hair. Alice's lips tightened as she walked back to her dresser and picked up her hairpins. Quickly, she coiled her hair into a severe knot and rammed her hat on her head. Just because she was having lunch with Lancelot didn't mean she had to act like a fool. What had gotten into her anyhow?

"See you tonight," she called to Mrs. B as she went out the door.

Thirty minutes later she was in her office, dictating Lancelot's contract to Linda.

"How should I type his name? Just 'Lancelot'?" Linda asked.

"Add a provision that he can sign as 'Lancelot' if he wants. His lawyer can co-sign. We can also handle payments through the lawyer."

The morning flew by as Alice immersed herself in work. The job of running her own television commercial production company was demanding, but she loved it. By the time she arrived at Locke-Ober she had completely dismissed her encounter on the lobster boat with Lancelot as a freakish happening. She was a fully restored Alice Spencer, all business.

Eduardo Velasquez was already seated in the elegantly paneled, Victorian-style downstairs dining room. He rose as the maître d' led her to the table and took her hand. "Alice. How good to see you."

His teeth flashed whitely below his small mustache as he bent over her hand and brushed it lightly with his lips. His English was spoken with a heavy Spanish accent so that "Alice" sounded soft and romantic, "Ahleese."

"I have good news for you, Eduardo. I found the perfect man, and I believe he will take the job. The only reservation I have is that he is . . ." She hesitated, searching for the right word. "Rough."

"Like a—how do you say it?—diamond in the rough?"

"Let's hope so, Eduardo. Anyhow, he won't have to do a thing but look fantastic in your clothes. And I believe he can manage that." Alice was delighted that she could talk about Lancelot in such a clinical manner.

Then he came through the door, and the impact of seeing him again socked Alice right in the stomach. He was wearing an old tweed jacket and a carelessly knotted tie with—of all things—blue jeans. On him, the unlikely combination looked like the latest fashion for discriminating men. He hailed her with a casual wave of his hand and sauntered over to their table.

"Eduardo Velasquez," Alice said when he reached them, "this is the man I was telling you about. Lancelot."

"You edited your comments, I trust," Lancelot said smoothly to Alice as he shook hands with Eduardo.

How Lancelot could manage to turn a simple introduction into a shambles was a mystery to Alice. Unconsciously, she stiffened, holding her back ramrod straight. She would not be rattled by this man today, she vowed silently.

"Tell me about your line of clothes," Lancelot said to Eduardo as he sat down.

Alice looked at him in surprise. She had him pegged as somebody who would do anything for the money. Now he was leaning toward Eduardo, listening with keen interest as the Spanish designer described his line. He didn't act very much like a lobster fisherman, she thought, but then she knew only one. Him.

"The designs are smart, debonair, semiconservative, but exciting," Eduardo was saying. "The careful structuring of each garment makes my line fit as no other does." When Eduardo became excited he talked with his hands. At the moment they were moving about like windmills.

"That sounds okay to me," Lancelot said. He laced his fingers behind his head, stretched his long legs out in front of him, and leaned back in his chair. "I wouldn't want to be seen on TV in anything kinky."

Eduardo looked at Alice for interpretation.

"Weird," she said.

"Exactly, Miss Spencer," Lancelot said. "And now can a starving fisherman eat, or do you plan to make me sign on the dotted line first?" As he spoke, he studied Alice closely and wondered why he hadn't noticed her eyes the day before. They were the clearest, most beautiful shade of blue-green he had ever seen. They were frank and honest too. The kind of eyes a man could trust.

"Does that mean you've decided to do the job?" she asked him.

"Can I trust you to hold up your end of the deal?" He leaned alarmingly close to her. He was so close that she caught a whiff of his woodsy after-shave.

That surprised her too. She had thought he would smell like fish all the time.

She shifted as far back in her chair as she could. Away from Lancelot. Somehow being this close to him took all the starch out of her bones. "Naturally, I will abide by the terms of the contract," she said stiffly.

"When you get all hot and bothered your eyes turn the color of the Mediterranean," he said softly.

"Nonsense." She pushed her glasses firmly against the bridge of her nose. Nobody had ever said such a thing to her before. How would he know the color of the Mediterranean anyhow? There was no use paying attention to anything this lobster fisherman said. "Shall we order lunch?"

"I don't know. Shall we?" he teased. "It's more fun to see how quickly an iceberg will melt."

Eduardo peered out from behind his menu, glanced quickly from one of them to the other, decided the conversation had nothing to do with him, and disappeared again.

"A moment ago you described yourself as starving." She fairly spat the words at him. Iceberg, indeed! She'd show him how fast an iceberg could crush a fisherman. "I'd suggest you eat, or you'll lose all those muscles and be useless to us as a model." That should hit him in the old pocketbook, she thought.

"Why, Miss Spencer," he drawled. "I didn't think you had noticed."

"It's my job to notice." She snapped the menu open and studied it as if she had never seen a menu before. She felt an urge to run a finger under her collar to release some of the heat, but she'd be damned if she'd give him the satisfaction of seeing that.

"Which do you recommend?" he asked. "The lobster Newburg or the shrimp thermidor?"

At last, she thought. He had decided to behave and conduct himself like a proper gentleman. She gave him a genuine smile. "Lobster." She placed her menu on the table and relaxed.

Lance's hand shot out and covered hers. Inclining his head to within only inches from her face, he whispered, "Had any problems with your blouse lately, Alice?"

She jerked her hand away and straightened her hat to remind herself that she was, in fact, sitting in a proper Boston restaurant, not rushing her way through a carnival's crazy house. "Are you insane?" she hissed.

"No, but you're melting."

"The only thing that's melting is the ice in your water glass. And it would behoove you to remember that I'm going to be your boss for the next few months."

"Yes ma'am," he said meekly. But he didn't look meek at all. Not the least little bit.

If he hadn't been perfect for the job, Alice would have dismissed him without batting an eyelash. She ordered her lobster Newburg and prayed that she would be able to get through the rest of the meal. Fortunately, Lance conducted himself like a lamb. She might even have decided he was charming if she hadn't known better.

He managed to fool Eduardo completely. By the time the meal was over the two of them were chatting like bosom buddies. Lance even spoke in Spanish with Eduardo, further astonishing Alice. The two men shook hands warmly as they parted outside Locke-Ober. "We will have a very good time together, my friend," Eduardo said. "You will make my clothes look even more wonderful, and I will show you my country. It is the best." He climbed into a waiting taxi and waved good-bye to them from the rear window.

"Charming man," Lance said to Alice.

"Yes, he is. It will be a pleasure to work with him."

He took her elbow, and smiled at her in a positively devastating way. "Your place or mine?"

Her vision blurred. Oh, Lord, she thought. Was he propositioning her?

"The contract," Lance added. "Remember?" He cast a bemused smile in her direction. He was accustomed to reactions from women, but he had never seen one quite like Alice's. He was intrigued.

Alice mentally kicked herself down the street and back. The next few months could very well prove to be the longest in her life. "My office," she said somewhat weakly.

"Do you have a car?"

"No. I don't like to drive in Boston. We'll have to take a cab."

It turned out to be the smallest cab she had ever set foot in. Lancelot took up the whole seat, and there was nowhere she could sit without brushing against his long legs. It was like being caught in an electrical storm. The hairs on her arms practically stood on end from so much shocking contact with the brazen fisherman.

He didn't seem to notice. Even when the cabdriver swerved around a corner and she had to clutch the door handle to keep from landing in his lap he acted as if nothing out of the ordinary was going on.

"Excuse me," she said when her knee brushed against his leg.

He merely lifted his eyebrows, and the corners of his mouth quirked upward. Thank heavens he refrained from making one of his wisecracks, she thought.

An eternity after leaving Locke-Ober the cab deposited them outside her office building. Alice managed not to suffocate while riding up with him in the elevator. By the time they reached the tenth floor, though, she had decided that wool was too hot for October. The next time she made a business date with Lance she'd wear something sensible, like seersucker.

Lance held the door for her and almost made her believe he was a gentleman as they entered her office. But she kept her guard up. He was totally unpredictable.

"Nice," he commented as he looked around, his gaze taking in the shiny mahogany desk, the Queen Anne chairs with their blue silk seat cushions, the light gray carpet, and the lush green ferns flanking a large window that looked out over the city. He noticed that the rooms had a tidiness that reflected its owner. He studied the trim woman across the room. It occurred to him that Alice Spencer had not once eyed him with predatory speculation. That alone put her in a class by herself. What was it about her, he wondered, that made her different? And why did that difference challenge him? His eyes were hooded as he waited with casual grace beside the desk.

Alice put her hat in the closet and moved swiftly to put a desk between herself and Lancelot. "I'm glad you approve of my office. And now, if you'll just look over this contract and sign in the two places that I've marked . . ."

His signature was a bold, black scrawl on the neat contracts. Just Lancelot. Nothing more. Carelessly, he flipped a business card onto the desk. "My lawyer. He'll handle everything."

Alice turned the card over. Just as she had suspected, his lawyer had an address in Charleston, South Carolina. Something more than curiosity stirred within her as she looked at the address. Could that be Lance's home? Did the man have roots there, or was Charleston just one of the cities he had passed through?

As she paper-clipped the card to the contract, the audacious signature caught her eye. There was something vaguely threatening about that signature, but she didn't know—didn't want to know— just what it was. Slowly, she lifted her gaze from the signature to the man who had put it there. "You're still calling yourself Lance, I see. Somehow I expected you to use your real name on the contracts."

"What is real and what is make-believe, Alice?" he asked softly.

She pondered the question. Was he a philosopher too? Lancelot continued to amaze her.

"Are *you* real, Alice?" His long arm reached across the desk, and he let his fingers trail down the side of her face. "Are you the prim Boston businesswoman you appear to be?" The fingers cupped her chin and forced her to look into his eyes. "Or is there a real woman hiding behind that proper exterior?"

With his fingers burning her skin, Alice was powerless to move. "How dare you say such things to me!" she said.

Lance laughed. "I dare, all right. I dare many things." His fingers lingered on her chin a moment longer, moving in soft circles against her skin. "Or have you forgotten?" Abruptly, he dropped his hand and walked out the door.

Alice stood very still, looking around her office. Her gaze touched each familiar piece of furniture. Nothing had changed except the feel of the place. She had been invaded. Lancelot had come into her workplace, her haven, and it was not the same anymore.

She touched the spot on her chin that he had touched and gazed thoughtfully down at his signature. Even his ink scrawl pulsed with life. Was that what she felt now in her office? Life vibrating around her?

Seeking to dispel such silly notions, she took out her notes on the shots she intended to make in Puerto Vallarta. She was soon immersed in her plans, but occasionally she reached up to touch her chin.

Three

Thirty-three Mt. Vernon was bedlam for a week as the trip to Puerto Vallarta was planned and discussed and anticipated. The office wasn't much better, with Linda forgetting where she had put her notepad as she dreamed of romantic Mexico, and the wardrobe mistress stewing about hot tamales and indigestion. Tom, Alice's assistant, provided a calming influence as he quietly made arrangements for the location filming.

Departure day finally arrived, and Alice somehow managed to get her excited family to the airport. Linda and the camera crew were already there, but Lancelot was nowhere in sight.

"Where is he? I'm dying to meet him," Linda said. She was wearing a shocking red jump suit that clashed with her hair.

"Patience, Linda." Alice smiled at her. "He'll be here if I have to go to that stinking lobster boat and drag him off by his hair."

Linda giggled. "I'll bet you would, Miss Spencer."

Mark tugged on Alice's skirt. "Aunt Alice, can I

stand at the window and watch the planes take off?"

"If Mrs. B will go with you." As Mark darted through the crowd Alice saw that Alex, the head cameraman, was walking toward her.

"A small personnel problem has developed, Alice." he said. "Bob is disgruntled because he's being paid less than Harvey. He's talking about walking out in Puerto Vallarta."

"Bob can be replaced," Alice said. "He's just a trainee. If there's any walking out, he's going to do it before we get to Mexico. I'll handle him, Alex." As she moved toward her rebellious cameraman, she scanned the airport for Lance. She might have known he wouldn't show up. He had been nothing but trouble from the first day she met him.

While she was settling the problem with Bob, their flight to Puerto Vallarta was announced.

"Everybody go ahead and board," she said to her crew. "I'll wait for Lance. If he doesn't show up, I'll find him or somebody else and come down on tomorrow's flight."

"How can you stay so *calm*, Miss Spencer?" Linda squeaked. "I'd be chewing my fingernails if I were in your shoes." In fact, Linda was chewing her nails.

"Worry never solved anything, Linda," Alice said. "I'll see you in Puerto Vallarta." She sat down on a vinyl seat and watched her crew board the plane. Mark waved until he had disappeared down the jetway to the waiting DC-10. She glanced at her watch. Two more minutes to takeoff. Anything could happen in two minutes.

"How nice of you to wait," a voice drawled. She looked up to see Lance strolling into the boarding area as if he were on his way to a Sunday picnic.

"You're late," she said as she stood and smoothed an imaginary wrinkle from her khaki skirt.

"You said that you had my boarding pass and the plane's still sitting there." That fantastic smile of his illuminated the airport. "How can I be late? Besides," he added as he took her elbow and escorted her to the gates, "rushing is bad for the heart."

"Do you practice medicine on that lobster boat of yours?" she asked scathingly, and jerked her elbow out of his grip. Why was he always touching? She didn't need to be guided down the ramp.

"Your tongue is just as sharp as I remembered. I do hope your attitude changes, or it will be a long flight to Puerto Vallarta."

"Forget it. My attitude is not your concern."

"Yes, ma'am," he said contritely. He smiled a dazzling smile that made the flight attendants beam as he boarded the plane. He looked virile and brawny and bronze and totally gorgeous walking down the aisle toward his seat. But not contrite. Not contrite at all.

Alice waved to Mark and Mrs. B, two seats back, and settled herself into the window seat. When Lance sat down beside her prickles of heat marched down her spine and a funny, fluttery sensation attacked her stomach. Maybe she had made a mistake choosing this fisherman, she thought. Maybe she should have settled for one of those cardboard men the model agency had. She pulled her notebook out of her briefcase and sat back in her seat. Was this what Heather had felt with men? she wondered. This vibrancy, this pleasant tingling? She had better be on her guard.

The plane taxied down the runway, climbed into

the air, then leveled off, heading west. Alice pretended an absorption she didn't feel in her notebook, hoping to discourage Lance from making conversation. After a few minutes of silence she sneaked a peek at him. He was leaning back in his seat, sound asleep. He'd probably had a late night out with some dizzy dame, she thought. Or maybe even two. She felt mildly irritated with him for falling asleep, and when she realized what she was feeling she became irked with herself. Good Lord! What difference did it make to her if he caroused all night and had to sleep it off the next day? He was nothing to her except a model.

While he was asleep she studied him boldly. For purely business reasons, of course. He would photograph beautifully, she decided as she looked at the fine planes of his cheeks, the aristocratic nose, and the sensuous mouth. Her palms became moist as she contemplated that mouth. What would it feel like pressed against her own? Her lips parted slightly.

Lance opened his eyes and looked straight at her. His smile started slowly at the corners of his mouth and spread all the way up to his blue eyes. He lifted one perfect brow and returned her stare.

Alice knew she was caught. His grin was so wicked he must surely know what she had been thinking. "I . . . I can never sleep on a plane," she said lamely.

"That's because you don't loosen up enough," he drawled pleasantly. "You're all starch and stiffness."

Her mind was so beguiled by his sensuous lips that she couldn't think of a suitably scathing reply. She would make sure she never sat next to him on a long plane ride again. She could feel all that starch and stiffness he talked about wilting. And it felt so good. Oh, Lord! she thought. What if she turned out to be like Heather? Pregnant and abandoned.

"Tell me about your business, Alice," he said. "How did you come to have your own company?"

"My business?" She sounded like Linda squeaking, she thought with disgust. The sane part of her mind stood back and scoffed at her. Pregnant and abandoned at her age? Even the brazen lobster fisherman took pity on her. He was changing the subject to save her further embarrassment.

"Your television production company," Lance said, proddingly.

Alice pulled herself together. "When I graduated from college I went to work for a large production company. I was more or less a glorified errand girl." Her voice sounded reasonably normal, she thought. If she could just make it to Mexico and get him on the opposite side of the camera from her, she'd be all right.

"I can't imagine you as anything except a boss," he said.

"I wasn't even a successful errand girl, apparently. I had worked there less than a year when the company experienced financial difficulties. I was one of the first ones they terminated."

Lance laughed heartily. "Whatever happened to good, old-fashioned 'fired'? 'Terminate' sounds like something that should be done with a spray gun and a strong insecticide."

Alice joined in his laughter. "I think it fell victim to modern English. Anyway, after I was fired I couldn't find a job. Nobody was hiring. So I started my own company."

"Wait a minute. I think I missed something in

there. You left out the best part of the story. The part about the brash young girl struggling through hard times, borrowing money when nobody wanted to lend it to her."

"It wasn't quite that romantic. I borrowed enough money, with my father as my security, to buy my own camera. I worked out of my home for a year and a half until I began to do a small amount of business and could afford to rent a small, one-room office and hire an assistant."

"No days of standing in the soup lines? No hearts and flowers and sad violins? Aw shucks, ma'am. I'm disappointed."

"I'm afraid not. I was just too young and too foolish to realize that I might fail, so my little company plodded along steadily, picking up customers at it went."

"And look at you now."

She ignored the compliment. "And what about you? I find you quite out of character as a lobster fisherman."

"How is that?" She could feel him pull away from her, as if he were drawing a shell around himself.

"You speak Spanish, and your English isn't so bad either, for a Southerner." She smiled to show that there was no intended sting in the words. As a matter of fact, she loved his Southern drawl. It made her think of moonlit nights on quiet verandas. "There is a certain refinement about you that I can't quite put my finger on."

"How many fishermen do you know?"

"Only you."

"I thought so. We're not all what we seem to be. My best pal on the lobster boat is an oncologist. He got sick of seeing people die of cancer, so he took to the sea. It's an ancient urge in men. Some call it wanderlust; others call it foolishness."

"And what about you? What did you leave behind?"

"I'm just a natural drifter."

"Don't you have a place you call home?" she persisted. For her it was more than idle curiosity or making conversation to pass the time away. She really wanted to know about this man, but she wasn't about to ask herself why. She was afraid of what her answer would be.

"Everywhere and nowhere," he answered evasively. It was obvious that he didn't like talking about himself.

"I'll bet you're a corporate president who got tired of all the pressure, or an engineer whose talents were overlooked, or maybe an undercover agent." Alice knew it wasn't like her to indulge in such fanciful talk. The sensible part of her decided that being 38,000 feet in the air had addled her brain. Or maybe it was Lance's smile.

"No need to try and make a silk purse out of a sow's ear, Alice," he said.

"A sow's ear? Can I take back what I said earlier about you having refinement?"

He grinned. "I thought you might." He stretched his long legs as far as the airplane seat would allow. "I'm just a simple man. All I require is good food, a roof over my head, and a good woman to warm my bed at night."

Alice swallowed nervously. How he continually managed to throw her slightly off kilter was beyond her comprehension. Her carefully ordered world seemed to be crumbling about the edges. "I see," she murmured. She turned hastily back to her notebook as if it contained vital information that required her immediate attention. She shoved her glasses firmly up on her nose and bent over the notes, frowning slightly in concentration.

Lance leaned over her casually, propping his elbows on the armrest between them, and studied the scene out the window. His face was only inches from hers, so close that she could see a small, crescent-shaped scar beneath his jawbone, barely visible through the close stubble of his beard. She sucked in her breath sharply between her teeth.

"Just admiring the view," he said.

She cut her eyes toward the window. She could see nothing except clouds, puffed and stacked together like row after row of sheep going to market. "Do you want to swap seats?" she offered.

"No. This is just fine." He continued to gaze out the window as if he were seeing the Taj Mahal for the first time and found the view fascinating. He leaned farther over, sliding his right arm off the armrest and letting it drop lightly into her lap.

The heat of it seared all the way through her khaki skirt, burned through her silk slip, scorched through her sensible cotton panties, and ignited a flame deep inside her body. The words in her notebook blurred. She looked at his wheat-colored hair and wondered wildly if his posture was calculated. Did he intend to make her one of those good women warming his bed at night? She swallowed convulsively and almost choked.

"Let your trays down if you want lunch, please." A flight attendant was standing in the aisle behind a cart. Alice looked at her as if she had come from another planet.

Lance sat up and obediently snapped down his tray. "I'm starving," he said.

Alice couldn't move. She wondered if she had somehow died and rigor mortis had set in.

Lance reached across and lowered her tray. "Hungry?" he asked.

She nodded, but didn't look at him.

A compact plastic tray was plopped efficiently onto her tray. Automatically, she tore off the wrap on the cutlery and napkin and took them from their bag. She tried a mouthful of food. It might have been green beans, but she didn't know for sure.

Beside her, Lance was chatting pleasantly with the flight attendant. Snatches of the conversation began to penetrate her fog. "Love to fly." "See places I couldn't see otherwise." "No. Never had any trouble." "Good pilots." "Yes, I will."

Yes, she will what? Alice wondered as she came out of her stupor and looked at the flight attendant. She was tall and willowy, with perfect olive skin and startling green eyes. Her auburn hair was carefully tousled, as if she had just stepped off a windy beach. She was everything Alice Spencer was not. She was like Alice's sister, the pretty one. She exuded a healthy sexuality.

Alice speared her rubbery chicken viciously. She felt ridiculous for thinking Lance had designs to get her into his bed. Why would he want somebody with ordinary brown knotted hair and glasses when there were women like that around? Alice didn't like to feel ridiculous.

"Is the food good?" Lance asked, turning to her.

Airplane food? she thought. Was he kidding? "Why don't you eat it and find out for yourself," she said curtly.

He got the message. They ate their meals silently, making no attempt at small talk. When the meal was over Lance thumbed through the magazine that was in the pocket of the seat in front of him and Alice went back to studying her notes. Lance, however, was not concentrating on the magazine. He was thinking about Alice.

He remembered the vulnerable look on her face when he had caught her staring at him earlier. He had found that glimpse of softness infinitely appealing, and was damned if he could figure out why. He also remembered the closed look on her face, as if she were shutting the door on her private self, when he had told her all he wanted was a good woman to warm his bed. He was fascinated by her, and wondered how long it would take to uncover all the facets of her personality that she kept so carefully hidden under her proper exterior. He didn't know why, though, he wanted to find the real Alice Spencer. Probably curiosity, he told himself.

For Alice, the remaining two hours of the flight crept along like six. Since they had traveled so far west, the sun was still high when they landed in Puerto Vallarta. As the passengers began to deplane, she told Lance to go ahead and meet the rest of the crew. She didn't feel like fighting the crowd, and waited in her seat until almost everyone else was off the plane. By the time she joined the crew, a beaming Eduardo, who had come to meet them at the plane, had Lance in tow and was introducing him around.

They claimed their bags, hired six taxis, and rode to the Hotel Camino Real on Banderas Bay. Mrs. B, Mark, and Linda rode in one taxi with Alice. Mark bounced around like a jumping bean, pointing at everything in sight and asking a million questions. Linda and Mrs. B carried on an avid conversation about Lance's merits.

"He's a dreamboat. I nearly swooned when he took my hand," Linda gushed.

"What I liked about him was the way he talked to Mark," Mrs. B said. "So natural. Like he loved kids." She gave Alice a significant look, then went on. "Mark really took to him too. I, of course, explained that you're Mark's aunt."

Oh, no, Alice thought. What if Mark got attached to Lance? She shook the thought off and concentrated on answering Mark's questions. She had had her fill of Lance Whatever-his-name-was for the day.

They reached Playa las Estacas and saw the hotel, its white stucco walls gleaming like jewels against the backdrop of the sapphire waters.

"Oh my," Mrs. B exclaimed. "I never expected anything so beautiful."

"Just like a picture book," Linda said.

Everyone helped to unload the luggage and equipment from the six taxis, and with the help of a couple of bellhops hauled it into the cool, tiled reception area of the Hotel Camino Real. Ceiling fans turned lazily, stirring a breeze.

A small, dapper man with a polished smile and a great, drooping mustache came from behind a massive, carved desk to dispense keys to his guests and send the bags to the right rooms. He wove in and out among the bags and cameras and tripods and people, and his polished smile became thin and nervous as he tried to deal with the unusually large crowd.

While Alice waited for the manager to reach her, she noticed a heavyset woman with crimped yellow hair passing through the lobby, leading a fat poodle on a leash. The noise of the crowd apparently made the poodle nervous, for he suddenly bolted, jerking the leash from his owner's hand and plunging straight into the middle of the crowd.

To Alice's horror, the trailing leash wrapped itself around her legs, yanking her down on top of her suitcase. Lance hurried to her side and extended a hand to help her up. Just then the fat lady rushed into the melee after her poodle. Alice cringed as the woman, round arms flailing like windmills and fat feet pumping along in red spike-heeled shoes, plowed into Lance, mowing him down like wheat. He fell heavily on top of Alice, grunting with the impact.

"*Dios mio!*" the manager cried.

"Somebody catch that damn dog." Alex yelled.

Mark was already in joyful pursuit of the culprit. With little-boy skill and cunning, he assessed the dog's intended direction, hid behind a potted palm, and captured the fat runaway with a swift jump.

"I got him! I got him!" he yelled as he held the wiggling poodle in his arms.

As the distraught manager began the tedious process of restoring order to the confusion, Alice looked up at Lance. "You can get off me now," she said. Lance's long legs were sprawled along the length of hers, pinning her to the floor, and his chest lightly brushed the tops of her breasts as he leaned on his elbows and watched the confusion with amusement.

"This makes the whole trip worthwhile," he said. "What a riot." He made no effort to move.

"You have a warped sense of humor. Get up." If he didn't get up soon, Alice thought, there was no telling what she would do. Her head was beginning to reel with the nearness of him.

"This is real comedy. Man in the process of being

man." He shifted his weight to his right elbow, fitting himself more comfortably along the curves of her body. "I'm not too heavy, am I?" He glanced at her stricken face. "I thought not." His eyes danced as he watched the manager and the owner of the poodle. They were now engaged in a heated argument. "I wonder who will win."

"Why don't you get up and take bets?" Oh, Lord! She was embarrassingly aware of the feel of the hard muscles of his legs and the shape of his maleness against her. Fortunately, everybody was too excited to notice what was going on on the floor.

Finally the argument was resolved. The fat lady won. She had the manager apologizing profusely to her and her dog.

Lance sat up and extended his hand to Alice. She took it. What else did she have to lose? she asked herself. She had lost her control, her decorum, and her sense of direction all in one day. Her glasses had been knocked from her face and had skidded across the tile floor when she fell. They winked at her from under a coffee table, but, she made no move to get them. It probably was best not to see what was going on anyway. She smoothed her skirt, and saw that both the manager and Mark were standing beside Lance.

"Will the *señor* and *señora* be staying in the same room with their son?" the manager asked.

"I don't know," Lance said, smiling wickedly as he turned to Alice. "What do you think, darling?"

To make matters worse, Mark grabbed Lance's hand. "Oh, goody. Do I get to room with him?"

Alice could have choked them both. She looked from one to the other. It was uncanny how much alike they looked. No wonder the poor confused man thought they were father and son. Mark had his mother's blond hair and blue eyes, hair and eyes just a shade lighter than Lance's.

"No," she said. "Mark will be staying with Mrs. B." She indicated the spry, gray-haired lady, who was watching them with a pleased smile on her face.

"You will show me how to dive? You promised," Mark said to Lance as Mrs. B led him away.

"Sure thing, sport," Lance said, then looked quizzically at Alice.

"I can't swim," she said tersely.

"If the *señor* and *señora* will follow me, please?"

"Oh, but we're not . . . I'm not . . ." Alice realized that she hadn't clarified their relationship to the manager. "We have separate rooms."

"Separate rooms?" The manager's mustache dropped even further at such a dreary prospect.

"Are you sure about this, darling?" Lance asked her. He was obviously enjoying the misunderstanding immensely.

"Will you quit calling me 'dahling'?" she snapped, imitating his Southern drawl. She was furious with him. She rued the day she had ever gone to the docks looking for a real man. She had gotten more than she bargained for.

"*Señora?*"

"It's *señorita*. He's not my husband and I'm not his wife and Mark is not our son."

""*Dios mio!*" The manager clapped his hands against his face and scurried to his desk to get another key.

"What a shame," Lance said. "I was looking forward to having you for a roommate."

"A woman to warm your bed?" she asked sarcastically.

"Perhaps." He took the key the manager handed him and disappeared into the cool vastness of the hotel.

Alice retrieved her glasses, then settled her belongings into her own room, checked on Mark and Mrs. B, and joined Eduardo in the lobby. They spent the rest of the day scouting locations, and afterwards had dinner at his home. Eduardo was pleasant company, and Alice found herself relaxing in his presence. Their business talk was interspersed with laughter and joking. The bold fisherman who called himself Lancelot faded into insignificance as she gave herself up to the immense pleasure of doing what she did best, conducting business.

Later that night Alice stood on her balcony overlooking Banderas Bay. She was wearing a white cotton nightgown, and her hair flowed loosely around her shoulders. The gentle night breeze caressed her skin. It was a night made for lovers, she thought dreamily.

Unbidden, Lance came to mind. What had he meant when he said "Perhaps?" Did that mean she was attractive to him as a possible lover? She had never felt attractive to the opposite sex. She had always been the one with the glasses and the brains. Heather had been the beauty, the one with a whole string of admirers. Even in college Alice had felt overshadowed by her older sister's beauty. Oh, sure, she had had her share of dates—Heather's rejects or the eggheads who would rather discuss Physics II than explore the pleasures of the flesh. The best Alice could remember, those hasty clenchings in the backseat of a car hadn't been all they were cracked up to be anyhow.

And then Heather had died. Six months later

Dad had given up and died, and Alice's whole world had changed. There simply had been no time for men. She had been too busy raising her nephew and keeping her head above water financially. During the past few years, of course, there had been men—men like Ralph, who were good company and good escorts, but nothing else. Nothing like Lance. Lance aroused delicious feelings inside her, feelings she had never experienced before. The scary part was that she liked them. She liked them very much. Oh, Lord, was she plunging into disaster? she wondered. Lance was a nameless, homeless man, a man whose avowed purpose was to have a woman to warm his bed. He was the very kind of gorgeous ne'er-do-well Heather would have chosen.

With the instinct for analysis that had made her a successful businesswoman, Alice looked at the problem. She was thirty years old. She had never been with a man and had never wanted to be with a man. Until now. She'd seen the destructive force men had been in Heather's life. But then, Heather was different. Something inside her had driven her to seek the wrong kind of man. Neither she nor Alice had had the guidance of a mother. Maybe that was why Heather had been the way she was, and perhaps that was why Alice had never blossomed.

She suddenly realized that her whole life up to this point had been a denial of everything Heather had been and everything she had done. Alice had never faced that before. She'd always thought her life was a carefully planned design of her own choosing. It shook her to think that she had been guided by negatives.

She lifted her soft hair and let the breeze cool her

neck. She had the drowning realization that she wanted to know what it was like to be in the arms of a man. Not just any man's arms, but his. The vagabond fisherman.

Four

Lance lounged carelessly against the dock railing, waiting for the next footage to be shot, and watched Alice at work. She moved around the cameras and equipment with self-confident ease, saying a quiet word here, soothing a ruffled feather there. He admired the way she efficiently brought order out of chaos.

Although her clothes were the same simple tailored garments he was accustomed to seeing her wear, she seemed different today, less starchy, more vulnerable. She was wearing sunglasses against the glare of the sun off Banderas Bay, and as she stopped to check the focus on one of the cameras the wind whipped a soft curl out of her severe topknot. A smile curved his lips as he thought what it would be like to tuck that curl behind her ear. The smile widened as he pictured her reaction.

He watched as she walked over to Linda. Her beige linen slacks and matching silk blouse looked as fresh and crisp as they had when she had first walked onto the beach two hours before. Her neatness was in sharp contrast to Linda's appearance. She resembled a small, harried Pekingese as she hopped frantically between cameramen and wardrobe mistress, alternately chewing the end of her pencil to shreds and wringing her hands.

"Just look at the size of these slacks, Miss Spencer," Linda wailed, holding up a pair for Lance's next shot. "Somebody has made a terrible mistake. They're big enough for you and Lancelot both." Too late, she realized what she had said.

Raising stricken eyes to her boss, she hastily tried to make amends. "Oh, I didn't mean . . ." She stopped in midsentence, and her mouth dropped open in amazement. Miss Spencer was looking toward Lancelot, smiling. It wasn't so much that she was smiling, it was the *kind* of smile on Miss Spencer's face that caused Linda to snap her pencil in half. It was a smile that she called dreamy-eyed bedroom, and it was as foreign on Miss Spencer's face as was a polar bear in Florida.

Aware that Linda was staring at her, Alice tore her gaze away from Lance. "A few pins strategically placed should do the trick," she said. "You worry too much, Linda. I want you to relax and enjoy your stay here. Remember, for every problem there is a solution." Except for problems of the heart, Alice added to herself.

She then shrugged away the thought and tried to concentrate on her work. Lancelot was even more impossibly handsome in the sunshine, with the blue waters of the bay gleaming at his back, than he had been when she first saw him on the lobster boat. She had no illusions about her own looks, though. In the broad light of day her romantic longings of the night before seemed ridiculous, and more than that, impossible. She was a gambler, willing to take risks in her business. Matters of the heart were quite another thing, however. She didn't even know the rules of the game in that area, let alone its finer gambling techniques.

"Take those pants to him," she said to Linda, and nodded in Lance's direction, "and tell him we'll be ready to shoot the next sequence in five minutes."

"Me!" Linda squeaked. "You mean I get to go over there and give him his pants? That mouth-watering hunk over there? Me, Miss Spencer? Me and Lancelot's pants?"

Alice laughed. "You're beginning to sound like a broken record, Linda. Now scoot." She almost envied the younger woman's outright adoration of her model. Under the pretext of checking a camera angle, she watched Lance through the lens. Linda was only halfway right, she decided. He was not just mouth-watering—he looked good enough to eat with a spoon. If only she had the nerve to pick up the spoon!

Lance disappeared from the view of her camera, and she lost herself in adjusting the distance and light settings. Although she now had a crew to do the camerawork while she concentrated on the directing, she missed the excitement of doing it all, the early days when she had worked with a camera slung around her neck, pencils tucked behind her ears, and notebooks spilling out of her briefcase.

"See anything you like?"

She jumped at the sound of Lance's voice behind her. "Don't do that," she snapped as she whirled around. When she saw him any other words she might have said floated out to sea, borne along by the mighty gasp of consternation that escaped her lips.

Lance was smiling, holding the enormous pants around his trim hips with one hand, and his bronze chest was as naked as the day he was born. "What are you going to do about my pants, Miss Spencer?" He watched the color creep into her face and wished that she wasn't wearing sunglasses so that he could see her eyes. He remembered the way they changed from aqua crystal to turbulent sea-blue when she was flustered.

Alice could scarcely focus her eyes as she gazed at the mat of golden hair that covered his chest and tapered to a slender line at the waistband of his pants. She thought she might faint at this close-up view she was getting of all this maleness.

"Alice?" Lance inquired politely. He was having a hard time holding back his laughter.

She shook her head and lifted her dazed face to his. "What?"

"My pants?"

"They're too big," she pronounced, robotlike. She wondered vaguely why she and Lance were the only two people left standing on the earth and where everybody else had disappeared to. Not that she minded, of course, for she was seriously considering floating into his arms and flying to the moon.

"What are you going to do?" he asked.

"About flying?" She wrinkled her brow and pondered whether he had ever flown to the moon before. She guessed not, or he wouldn't be standing there moving his mouth. What was he saying?

Mattie Grover, the wardrobe mistress, arrived, out of breath and disgruntled from her walk across the sandy beach. "Here!" she bellowed as she plopped a box of pins into Alice's numb hand. "You pin him up." She wiped her partridge-plump face with the back of her hand. "Damned sand and heat. I feel like a hot tamale." She favored Lance with a glare. "I'm taking a break with a tall glass of lemonade and I don't want to be bothered with pants!" Having said her final words on the subject, she marched back across the sand to the temporary dressing room, a gaily striped tent.

Alice felt as if she had just had a bucket of cold water dashed in her face. Mattie was like that. Nobody ever crossed her, and she was too good at her job to be replaced by a sweeter-tempered soul.

Looking from the pin box clutched in her hand to Lance, holding onto his pants, Alice snapped to attention. She had a commercial to do, and Lord only knew how much time she had already wasted in her catatonic state. "Turn around," she ordered Lance in what she hoped was a reasonably steady voice.

He obediently did as he was told. Lance felt her hands tremble against his back as she inserted the first hesitant pin into the top of his pants. He was sorely tempted to turn his head so that he could watch her face. After all the worldly wise and bold women who had brazenly caressed his flesh, Alice's timid touch was a refreshing change.

"Careful back there," he said with a straight face.

Gingerly, she lifted the loose fabric between two fingers, biting her lower lip as she worked. "I'm being as careful as I can. Hold still." Perspiration popped out on her brow as she tried to fit the pants to his hips with as little contact as possible with the bronzed flesh beneath. She had no doubts whatsoever that he was dark gold from the top of his head to the tips of his toes. With some long-buried, primitive instinct, she knew that he was the kind of man who would unabashedly go nude when he had the chance, letting the sun worship his magnificent body.

Forgetful of the task at hand, she drove a pin home, scoring his flesh.

"Ouch!"

She lifted her hands away from his pants as if she had been shot. "I'm sorry. Did I hurt you?"

"No. I meant to donate blood today."

The teasing remark helped to dispel the tension that had wrapped tightly around her. "Then perhaps I should stick you again."

"Not without anesthesia."

"Sorry. I'm fresh out. You'll just have to grin and bear it." With his back turned to her, it was easier for her to think of him as just another model. Willing herself to focus on her work, she quickly completed the fitting task. It was, after all, a job she had done countless times over the years. She smiled, proud of herself for having overcome her temporary insanity. "All done," she announced.

Lance turned around slowly and smiled down at her with a lazy, cat-stole-the-cream smile. "About that anesthesia." His head dipped forward and his tongue flicked briefly across her lips. "That's been known to work wonders."

He was gone so quickly that Alice thought she had dreamed his touch. Putting a hand to her lips, she felt the moisture still clinging there and groaned. Just when she thought she had a firm grip on her composure, Lancelot shot it all to hell and back. Maybe she, too, should disappear into the dressing tent with a glass of lemonade and let

Mattie direct the commercials. The way things were going, she was batting zero, and Mattie at the helm could only be an improvement.

Clearing her throat, Alice pushed her glasses firmly back up to the bridge of her nose. "Look sharp, everybody. We're ready for another take."

Fortunately for her, Lance behaved like a lamb for the next hour, posing with the uninhibited charm of a natural model. As the camera whirred behind her, capturing Lance in the exotic setting, Alice knew that these would be some of the best commercials she had ever done. She wrapped up the morning's shooting, and they broke for lunch, a catered affair set up under a large tent on the beach.

Lance slid onto a folding metal chair beside her, his plate piled high with food. "You're good, you know."

"Thanks. So are you." Alice determinedly kept her attention on his face, trying to keep her wandering eyes from dwelling too long on the parts of him that were left uncovered by his cutoff jeans and mesh football jersey.

"Have you ever modeled before?" she asked.

"Not for money."

She nearly choked on her guacamole salad. "Not for money" conjured up all kinds of pictures, most of them X-rated.

Lance thumped her on the back, grinning. "You have to be careful of these hot Mexican foods. They'll get you every time."

She glared at him over the top of her glass of lemonade. "It's not the food. It's you."

"I'm sorry," he said with a poker face. "I'll use mouth-to-mouth resuscitation since you don't approve of back-thumping." He leaned threateningly close.

"Don't you dare."

"Do you ever?"

"Do I ever what?"

"Do you ever dare?"

Ice rattled against the sides of her glass as she turned from him and set the glass on the table. The man was a sorcerer, she thought. Of course she didn't dare. Daring meant opening oneself up to all kinds of possibilities. Daring meant flying-to-the-stars joy and plummeting-to-hell pain. Daring meant opening the private doors of the soul and entrusting another person with its secrets. Daring meant the giving of something precious at the risk of losing it forever—or of having it returned a hundred fold.

She stood quickly to leave, chastising herself for having ever pictured herself in this man's arms. She wasn't ready to risk her heart on a dare.

"Alice." A bronze hand snaked out and captured her wrist. "Don't go. Stay and talk to me."

"Why?" She gave him an icy look.

"I want to know you," he said simply.

In the biblical sense? flashed into Alice's mind, and for an instant her mask slipped out of place. Quickly, she righted it. "You want to amuse yourself with me." She stood with quiet dignity, not trying to release her arm from his grip.

A look of admiration crossed Lance's face as he gently slid his hand from her wrist. Caution was strong in him as he looked up at Alice. If he wasn't careful, this little game he was playing could backfire. He sensed within this woman strength and dignity and courage, traits he had not often seen in people during his wanderlust years.

"Stay, Alice. I'll behave."

Something in the little-boy sincerity of his voice reminded her of Mark. Retrieving her lemonade, she sank back into the chair. Besides, she argued with herself, moving to another chair would cause speculation among the crew, and she was discreet to the nth degree.

"Tell me about Mark," Lance said, shifting from the ridiculous to the mundane without batting an eyelash.

"I'm Mark's legal guardian. My sister, Heather, was killed in an accident when he was a year old."

"You're doing it again," he teased lightly.

"What?"

"Leaving out the best part. The way you did on the plane. Somehow I think there's a long story of grief and pain and struggle that I'm not hearing."

"Caring for Mark has been more joy than struggle. And I've had Mrs. B to help me."

"Is Mark's father living?"

"Yes."

"And?"

"He removed himself from the picture when he abandoned my pregnant sister. Nobody knows where he is." Unconsciously, she tightened her grip on the long-suffering glass.

Lance digested this new bit of information about Alice, the glimmer of fear that had shown itself briefly when she spoke of her abandoned sister. He felt as if he had been given a wedge with which to pry open that closed door. Boldly, he plunged ahead on his quest, ruefully aware that curiosity sometimes killed the cat.

"What are you afraid of, Alice?"

The best defense against an unwanted question was another question, she decided. "What are you running from, Lancelot?" She placed deliberate emphasis on his fictitious name.

"Touché." He stood up and stretched like a lazy cat. "I believe I'll follow suit of the wise natives and indulge in a siesta."

She gave him a Mona Lisa smile. "Be ready for filming again at three." She watched as he crossed the beach to a blanket spread in the shade of the camera equipment van. There was more to him than met the eye, she thought. And that was saying a mouthful. If any more of him met the eye, she'd have to wear blinders.

The sun was still high when they resumed filming. Alice judged that she had time for the swimsuit commercial before the sun changed too much. Snapping orders with an efficiency she didn't quite feel, she readied the set. She wanted to catch the perfect angle of sunlight behind Lance's back.

"Miss Spencer!" Linda squealed as she hurried across the sandy beach. "That new makeup girl dropped a bottle of oil into the middle of Eduardo's pants . . ." Linda stopped and placed her hands over her heaving chest, gulping for breath. "You know, the ones we used in this morning's commercial. The ones you had to pin on Lancelot. The wheat-colored linen—"

"I know the pants, Linda," Alice said, trying to curb her impatience. "What happened?"

Linda's eyes were round with awe as she recounted the doings of the wardrobe mistress. "Mattie sent her packing. Said she had never seen such a clumsy-fingered goat in her life. That's what she called her, Miss Spencer, a goat."

"Someday Mattie is going to overstep her bounds," Alice muttered. "Where did Jeanette go? I'll have a talk with her."

"She's probably in South America by now, the way she was flying when she left here."

Alice gazed out across Banderas Bay, pondering the dilemma. "I'll talk with Jeanette tonight. You'll have to fill in for her."

"Me?" Linda clutched her notepad to her chest.

"Of course. This shot is very simple. All I want is a little oil rubbed on Lancelot's chest and shoulders so the sun will glisten on him. And maybe a dab or two on his hair," she added.

"*Me?* Me rub oil on that . . . Me touch that . . . Have you *seen* his chest, Miss Spencer?"

Alice couldn't hide her smile. If Linda squeaked up one more octave, she'd be off the scale, she thought. She knew how Linda felt, though. She had felt the same way this morning, pinning up Lance's pants. It was a cross between riding on a roller coaster and having Fourth of July fireworks set off under your feet. "Go ahead, Linda. We need to get this shot while the sun is right. And besides," she added cajolingly, "you *are* the one who called him a dreamboat."

"That was before I saw him naked—" She stopped, her face scarlet. "I mean, without his shirt. Dream cruise ship is more like it. I can't, Miss Spencer."

Alice glanced up at the angle of the sun and back to her distraught secretary. "Very well, Linda. I'll do it myself."

Feeling like a Christian going into the lion's den, Alice crossed to the dressing tent and entered.

"It's about time somebody with some sense showed up," Mattie said, uncrossing her arms from her ample bosom. "I don't have all day to lollygag with a flaky, mule-headed pig who ruins the wardrobe." She swept grandly past her boss. "I'm going to get a glass of refreshment before I turn into an enchilada. You can finish up here, Alice." Nobody except Mattie called the boss "Alice." Turning in the tent opening, she flung one last word over her shoulder. "If you ask me, and nobody has, Jeanette left her brains at the hotel this morning." Hands on hips, she glared at her boss and Lance.

Alice heaved a resigned sigh. She knew Mattie's grizzly-bear mood. There was nothing to do except wait for it to pass.

Lance, however, walked over to Mattie and casually draped his arm around her shoulders. "You deserve a break, Mattie. I've never seen a wardrobe mistress do a better job than you. Last year in Paris I had the good fortune to watch some shooting of the Givenchy collection. They would have been thrilled with somebody like you."

To Alice's amazement, Mattie's face was transformed from glaring to gleaming. "You don't say? Paris, huh?"

"Paris. And not a single person there with your talent."

Alice stood transfixed. Lance seemed as genuine and sincere as the president of the United States. She was so fascinated by his diplomatic maneuverings that she forgot her awesome task.

Mattie burst out laughing. "You don't look Irish, but you're full of blarney. I wish somebody would figure a way to melt you down and put you in a tonic. You're good for what ails me."

Lance playfully chucked the side of her cheek. "Nothing ails you except a little old-fashioned case of grumpiness. Why don't you go out there and find

Jeanette? She needs a shoulder to cry on. She got a 'Dear Jeanette' phone call from her boyfriend this morning."

"Why didn't she just say so in the first place? Poor little darlin'. If there's anything I can't stand it's a man who fritters around with your feelings and then goes off and ditches you like yesterday's leftovers." She drew herself up with importance and patted Lance's cheek. "You're pure gold. The solid, gen-u-ine article."

"Be gentle with Jeanette. She needs you."

"She won't know me from a lamb." Mattie sashayed happily out of the tent.

"How did you *do* that?" Alice asked. She believed that what she had witnessed was nothing short of a miracle. Who was this Lancelot, and why was he wasting his diplomatic talents posing as a model? she wondered.

"Mattie needed a little coaxing."

"That was more than a little coaxing. Nobody has ever been able to talk Mattie down from her high horse. And how did you know about Jeanette?"

"I saw her crying this morning. She confided in me."

"Just like that? She confided in a stranger?"

Lance dismissed this interesting tidbit with a shrug. "Beats me."

Completely forgetting the naked, golden chest in her admiration for the way he had handled the problem with Mattie and Jeanette, Alice prodded gently. "Where did you learn such smooth public relations tactics? You knew just how far to take the flattery, when to use humor, and when to appeal to Mattie's sympathies."

His face became unusually animated. "Back home in South Carolina—" He stopped abruptly, surprised at himself. He had almost revealed a part of his past to this woman. What was there about Alice, he wondered, that made him want to share his thoughts? He was uncomfortably aware that he was rapidly losing his grip on his no-involvement policy. "Here and there," he said nonchalantly. "What about that oil?"

"The oil?" she asked vaguely.

"Yes. The oil that you're going to generously slather on my body." He grinned, and then seeing her stricken face, temporarily repented of his wickedness. "Where did you find Mattie?"

Swallowing nervously, Alice focused her attention on the body she was supposed to slather, then quickly wished she hadn't. Her tongue clung to the dry roof of her mouth, and she tried not to gape at Lance in his swim trunks. God had played a cruel trick when He had fashioned that gorgeous, golden body and then put it in the way of an unsuspecting innocent like herself, Alice decided. It was a sin, a downright sin, to be expected to rub oil on that body without fainting. Poor Linda. No wonder she had been hysterical.

Faking a nonchalance she didn't feel, Alice picked up the bottle of baby oil. "I found Mattie while I was filming in Texas four years ago. She's unsinkable, unflappable, and unshakable. Everybody is scared to death of her . . . including me." She noted with satisfaction that her voice shook only slightly.

"I doubt that. I have the distinct feeling that you could back down a wounded bull elephant if you set your mind to it." He watched her face turn pink with the compliment. It was odd how heart-tugging that blush was. If he wasn't careful, he'd find himself more involved than he meant to be.

Quickly, he got on safer ground, and looked pointedly at the bottle of oil. "Fun-and-games time, Miss Spencer?"

With alacrity, she recovered from his compliment. She had to watch being taken in by his smooth talk. "You do fun and games on your own time," she said tartly. She was proud of her quick comeback. Maybe there was hope for her after all. "I want you to rub this oil lightly across the tops of your shoulders and in random spots on your chest and back."

"How random?" His teeth flashed whitely in his bronze face as he smiled at her.

Alice considered Lance's question, and her face flushed. She wasn't about to name that golden chest and that perfect back, not to mention those wonderful shoulders. Her hands fluttered vaguely in the air. "Oh, just here and there."

Lance smiled to himself. Dear Alice. Tough as nails when it came to business and a babe in the woods when it came to matters of the flesh. The idea pleased him, and damned if he could figure out why. "I'm afraid you'll have to show me, ma'am," he drawled. "Besides, I can't reach my back."

She had to stop and consider whether or not she was actually breathing. Clenching and unclenching her hands to stop their trembling, she took a step toward Lance. "Hand me the bottle and turn around," she said softly.

Telling herself that she was thirty years old, for goodness's sake, and not sixteen, she walked around him to that broad back, viewing it as if it were a rope and she had been sentenced to hang. He was just an ordinary man, made up of muscle and bone, she told herself. There was no need to

approach his shining flesh with weak-kneed adoration. No need whatsoever. Then why did her legs
keep trying to buckle?

She lifted one hesitant hand and carefully
smoothed oil across the back of his shoulders. The
first contact with Lance's smoothly muscled bare
back sent a shock wave that washed over her body
and nearly knocked her off her feet. She made a
strangled sound and forced herself not to jerk her
hand away from his skin.

"Did you say something?" Lance inquired
politely.

"Ho . . . I said, 'hold still.' "

"Did anybody ever tell you that your touch is like
silk?"

"No." She barely breathed the word as her hands
dreamily explored the smooth texture of his skin.

"Well, they should have." He cast an amused
glance over his shoulder. "While you're back there,
could you scratch my back? Right below that left
shoulder."

There was no response from Alice. She had
entered a dreamworld where nothing existed
except her hands and Lance's golden back.

"Did you know that Cinderella was actually an
ugly old witch and the Prince was secretly in love
with the fat stepsister?"

Still no response from Alice. She was the moth
and Lance the flame. Giddily, she plunged to her
destruction.

"Have you heard that Little Bo Peep didn't lose
her sheep? They joined the army so they could
wear camouflage green."

All was quiet. Alice was now spinning, spinning
through the air on a shiny golden carpet. A carpet

that bore a strong resemblance to Lance's muscled back.

"Alice? Paging Miss Alice Spencer."

Shaking her head, she came slowly out of her stupor. "What?"

"My back's about ready for the barbeque. What about the front?"

"The front?" She lifted her hands from his back and her eyes gradually came back into focus. "You can do the front."

Lance spun around and captured her oily hands in his. Placing them on his chest, he began a sensuous movement across his skin. "No need to waste the oil," he said with a smile.

"What oil?" She considered it a major miracle that she could speak.

"On your hands."

"Of course." Empires could have been built in the eternity that her hands touched his warm, sun-worshiped chest.

Lance looked down at her face, open and vulnerable, and suddenly he was filled with a fierce desire to protect her. The feelings startled him, for he had thought them lost many thousands of miles ago.

The kind of women he had met over the years had been too eager and too brash, ready to tumble into his bed at the crook of a finger. Alice was different. She was shy and prim in an old-fashioned way that he found appealing. She reminded him of his grandmother, that beguiling matriarch, delicate as porcelain, ephemeral as a butterfly, who had an inner core of tempered steel. Nanna could have turned Sherman back from the burning of Atlanta, and would have made him smile while he was retreating. Lance would have walked through fire for her.

Gently, he took Alice's hands from his chest. "Are you ready to shoot the commercial?" he asked.

She drew a shuddering breath. "Yes."

For the rest of the afternoon the normally stiff and proper Alice Spencer wore a slightly glazed look.

Mark bounced up and down on the edge of Alice's bed as she and Mrs. B talked about the day's events.

"Mark made friends with everybody in the hotel today," Mrs. B said, taking grandmotherly pride in all his accomplishments. "Before you know it he'll be speaking Spanish like the locals. And how was your day?"

Alice held up her five-year-old swimsuit, eyeing it critically. It was a sedate one-piece with a modestly scooped back and a demure front. Functional was the word for it.

"Fine," she said. She knew her answer wouldn't satisfy Mrs. B.

It didn't. "Fine? That's all you have to say after spending an entire day with Lance?"

Alice disappeared into the bathroom with her swimsuit so that she could change . . . and so that Mrs. B couldn't see her face. She thought it might break from the enormous effort of holding it straight. What she wanted to do was smile and swoon and sigh and maybe shed a tear or two. It had been that kind of day.

She neatly folded her robe and stepped into her swimsuit. "It was just business, Mrs. B," she called through the bathroom door. She hoped her nose wouldn't grow two inches from such a lie. Never had business been so unbusinesslike.

"I read the other day in *Dr. Zhivago*—or was it Dr. Kildare?—that a woman in love gets a flushed look. You had that look when you came back."

"You read too much." Alice adjusted the swimsuit straps.

"I know what I saw."

"Well, you saw wrong."

"Lancelot is wonderful. Reminds me of my Hugh."

"Lancelot isn't even his name."

"Names aren't important."

"I give up." She heard Mrs. B's pleased chuckle. Alice looked in the mirror and debated briefly with herself about leaving her hair loose. Who was she kidding? With her less than ample chest, she would resemble a boy scout if it weren't for the swimsuit's built-in bra. The pale blue suit looked like it had come over on the Mayflower, and she wasn't exactly pinup girl of the month. Shoving her glasses firmly on her nose, she joined Mark and Mrs. B. Her nephew was engrossed in a television program.

"You have a beautiful figure, Alice," Mrs. B said.

"I'm flat-chested."

"A model's figure. Slim and elegant. It's a shame to hide so much of it under that old menopause blue suit."

"What?" Alice figured Mrs. B rivaled Mattie for unique turns of phrase.

"That old washed-out, don't-look-at-me-I-feel-frumpy blue. What you need is a bright red bikini."

Alice laughed. "No thanks." Turning to her nephew, she said over the sound of the TV, "Are you ready, Mark?"

"Yippee!" He caught his aunt's hand and bounced along beside her. At the door, he turned to look back at Mrs. B. "Are you coming, too, Mrs. B?"

"No. I have a book to read. By a Dr. Jekyll—or is it Doolittle?" She waved them out the door. "Have fun."

The first person Alice saw at the swimming pool was Lance. He was poised on the diving board, and a retinue of scantily clad bathing beauties were oo-ing and ah-ing from poolside. Whirling quickly away from the scene, Alice chose a chair as far from the bright swimming pool lights as she could get without hiding in a potted palm.

She tried not to look at the diving board as she cautioned Mark to stay in the shallow end of the pool, but her attention was suddenly riveted as that Greek god's body poised briefly in the air, then sliced the water.

"Did you see that, Aunt Alice? Wow! That's Lance, and he's going to teach me to dive like that."

Before she could stop him, Mark ran to the edge of the pool and shouted, "Hey, Lance! Over here!"

The sleek blond head turned their way, and Alice melted inside her sedate suit as Lance shot them a brilliant smile. With quick, clean strokes, he cut through the water. Glistening wet, he rose from the pool and lifted Mark in his arms. "Hey, buddy. I've been looking for you."

Mark hugged his neck and then slithered down. "Are you really going to teach me to dive like that?"

"Sure thing. But we'll have to start small and work our way up." He made his way toward Alice's chair as he spoke. With the casual grace of a leopard, he settled into the chair beside her. "Hello, Alice," he drawled.

She wondered if the lilting, drawn-out way he said her name was calculated to turn her into a helpless lump of clay. If so, he had succeeded. Alice, who wouldn't shrink from a stampeding herd of buffalo, tried to disappear into the back of her chair. Thank goodness Mark's chattering covered her discomfiture, she thought.

"Are you ready, Lance? Can we go now? Bet I can beat you to the edge of the pool."

"You run along, Mark. I'll join you in a minute." Lance gave him a playful pat on the backside as he scooted off.

"Stay in the shallow end," Alice called after him.

"Hey, he'll be okay," Lance said. "He swims, doesn't he?"

"Yes, but . . ."

Lance saw the quick flash of anxiety in her eyes. She recovered so swiftly that the ordinary observer would never have noticed.

"I'm a fussbudget about the water." She laughed at herself, a quick sound without mirth. "I don't swim, you know. It's hard not to pass my phobia on to him."

"There's more to it than that, I think." He looked at the carefully prim woman in the sedate swimsuit and wondered again what was beneath that cool exterior. Until now he had toyed with her out of instinct and habit, out of a restless need to be doing something—anything—different. He had thought of himself as being on a quest to unlock the door to her private self. Suddenly she was more than a toy, more than a quest: She was a challenge, maybe the biggest challenge of his long and jaded career.

She had the quiet dignity of a madonna, he thought, and the cool aloofness of a princess. She had grit and spunk and a keen head for business. His gaze traveled down the length of her slim body, taking in the narrow waist, the softly curving hips, and the long, shapely legs. Nice, compact, and neat. But also remote, out-of-reach, like a wonderful package that had been sent to the wrong address and had to be stored on the shelf unopened.

As he accepted the challenge with an enigmatic smile and a curious quickening of his pulse, he reached across the small space that separated them and, with one finger, traced a burning path down the side of her cheek. "Don't go away, Alice." And he was gone.

Alice held her breath until he dived into the pool and surfaced beside Mark. She expelled a shuddering sigh and lifted her hand to her cheek, trying to hold the warm feeling of him against her skin. It must be the moon, she decided, glancing up at the pale sliver that was just visible in the early evening sky. Otherwise why would she be possessed by this strange longing to be in Lance's arms?

Mark's laughter floated to her across the pool, and she watched the two of them playing in the water. The blond heads bobbed a few feet apart, and identical smiles lit their faces. From the looks of them, she suspected that Lance was having as much fun as Mark.

Strange, she thought, that a man without a home, a man without roots, would take so much pleasure in the company of a child. Strange and curiously heart-tugging. Was it possible that the vagabond fisherman was not the debonair philanderer he seemed to be? With computer efficiency, her mind reached back to the day he had come to her office to sign the contract. He had dropped a clue then: What is real and what is make-believe? he had asked. Alice Spencer had to find out.

Smiling, she leaned back in the lounge chair and contentedly watched her nephew.

"Don't they make a pair?" she heard a voice suddenly say. She looked up to see Mrs. B standing beside her, beaming at Lance and Mark.

"You startled me," Alice said. "I didn't hear you come up."

"Obviously. You had your mind on something else."

"Now, Mrs. B, don't start that."

"Who? Me?" She was the picture of innocence. "I've come to take Mark up to bed."

"You needn't have bothered. I'll do it."

Mrs. B's face showed that she thought that suggestion ranked right up there with trying to climb the Matterhorn without a rope. "And waste an evening under the Mexican stars with you-know-who? I won't hear of it." As she hurried toward the pool to fetch Mark, she called back over her shoulder, "This is a night made for romance, Alice. Grab it before it gets away." With lightning speed, she hauled her charge from the pool and trundled him off to bed.

Alice rose to follow them, but was stopped by a long, wet arm. "Going somewhere?" Lance asked. She looked up at him. Droplets of water glistened on his smooth skin.

"Yes. To bed."

A slow, lazy smile lit his face. "What a wonderful idea, Alice." The wet arm slid around her waist, and he pulled her shockingly close.

Was that the pounding of the surf, Alice wondered, or her own blood roaring in her ears? "You're impossible."

"You're kissable." With expert ease, he maneuvered her around the end of the lounge chair and behind a potted palm. Cupping her face with his hands, he leaned close until his lips were only a hairbreadth away from hers. "Trust me, Alice," he whispered huskily. "This won't hurt one bit."

And then the world stopped turning on its axis and catapulated off into space, rocking with a dizzy speed that made Alice feel as though she might tilt off its edge. His lips against hers were warm and wonderful, tantalizingly sweet. They tasted, probed, teased, and finally possessed her completely.

Her arms lifted and wound themselves around his neck as her body strained to get closer to the magic feel of his. His wet legs pressed against hers, setting off a volcanic eruption inside her. Oh, Lord, she groaned silently, was this what she had been missing? This catch-the-brass-ring-on-the-carousel wonder? This flying-to-the-stars euphoria? She wanted to grab time in her fists and make it stand still while she caught up.

The slick dampness of his bare skin heightened the skyrocket sensations that coursed through Alice's body. She swayed in his arms, fitting herself to his muscled contours.

"Alice, Alice," he murmured as his lips left hers and roamed down the side of her arched neck.

With her head tilted back and fire licking through her veins, she looked up at the stars. They seemed closer and brighter, as if they had stepped down from the sky and turned up their beams to get a better look at the magic behind the potted palm.

Lance's hands moved to her swimsuit straps and hovered there. Then he lifted his head and looked into her eyes. "Ahh, Alice." It was a soft sound of regret, a gentle sigh like moonbeams caressing the sea.

Gently he turned her in his arms and pointed her in the direction of the hotel. "Sweet dreams," he whispered as she floated away in a daze.

His gaze followed her until she disappeared behind the heavy, carved doors. He stood very still, looking across the empty space where she had been. Something stirred deep inside him, something he had thought dead, buried under the avalanche of too many lonesome miles and too many wayfaring years. He *cared* about Alice. He really cared. He wanted to know her as a person, not just a lover. He wanted to know if she loved pizza and late movies. He wanted to know what made her laugh, what kind of music she liked, what kind of cereal she had for breakfast. "Well, I'll be damned," he said softly. Shaking his head in bewilderment, he turned on his heel and stalked off into the night.

Five

Alice woke up smiling, and the smile stayed with her through a hair-raising taxi ride to downtown Puerto Vallarta and a whirlwind day of gift-shopping and sightseeing with Mark and Mrs. B. Nothing could daunt her spirits today.

As the sun dipped into Banderas Bay she and her charges returned to the hotel, their arms laden with packages.

"Can I go swimming, Aunt Alice?" Mark asked.

"You can swim in Eduardo's pool while we're filming evening wear," she said. "Now scoot along with Mrs. B and change." She fitted the key into her lock and said to Mrs. B over her shoulder, "We'll be ready to leave in about an hour."

Stacking her packages neatly on the top shelf of the closet, Alice thought about the evening ahead. She wondered if Lance would find an opportunity to kiss her again. Had he enjoyed it the way she had? Probably not, a man of his experience. She shook her head impatiently. What had gotten into her anyhow, thinking about kisses instead of

doing a good job on the commercials? She rationalized that it had to be the city. Puerto Vallarta
reeked of romance.

She shrugged off her pleated linen skirt and her
cotton blouse and hung them in the closet,
smoothing the wrinkles as she did so. Her hands
ran across the dresses she had brought with her,
and she sighed. They were all sedate and sensible.
She wondered if her wardrobe would be different if
it weren't for Heather. Just this once she would
like to know the feeling of being dressed in something totally frivolous.

She decided on a jade silk sheath with high neck
and fitted sleeves. Reaching into one of her packages, she took out a bottle of bubble bath. *Noche
de las flores*—Night of the Flowers. She laughed.
What the heck, she thought. She was in Mexico.

Smiling, she entered the bathroom and mea-
sured a capful of bubble bath into the tub. The
sweet-smelling fragrance wafted up from the running water, and on impulse she dumped half the
bottle in. Call it madness. Call it moonstruck. Call
it anything. She was in a city of romance.

She soaked in the tub and hummed the only
Spanish song she knew, "La Cucaracha." Giggling
to herself, she decided that "The Cockroach"
wasn't in keeping with her hearts-and-flowers
mood. She would have hummed "Spanish Eyes,"
but she didn't know the tune.

She finally climbed out of the water, wrapped a
towel around herself, and looked at her face in the
mirror. The hint of fine lines around her eyes told
her that she wasn't a spring chicken anymore. Out
of habit, she lifted her head, pursed her lips, and
patted herself under the chin. Her philosophy was
that it never hurt to keep in shape.

In her bedroom, she plucked a pair of her sensible cotton panties out of a drawer. Did other women actually wear those minuscule bits of nylon held together with wisps of lace? she wondered. The kind she saw in window displays of stores with names like Naughty But Nice and Almost Hollywood. She smoothed her sedate underwear over her hips. If she wore those things, she'd be afraid to take a deep breath in public. What would happen if you had to cough? She pictured herself decked in a pair of Almost Hollywood panties, conducting a staff meeting. Right at the most crucial moment of the meeting she had a coughing fit and the panties fell to the floor. Alice began to giggle. Would she say, "Excuse me," and bend over to pick them up, or would she try to kick them under the table? She laughed so hard she had to sit on the edge of the bed to catch her breath.

She wiped the tears of mirth from her eyes with the edge of the sheet. Good grief, she thought, what was happening to her? It must be something they put in that bubble bath. She had never felt so giddy. Trying to recapture a sense of decorum, she walked to the closet, took out a silk sheath, and slipped it over her head. Every time she moved a wave of exotic fragrance drifted around her. She was beginning to regret the bubble bath. She smelled like a gardenia bush, for Pete's sake! Everybody was bound to wonder what had gotten into Alice Spencer.

She zipped her dress up and leaned in close to the mirror to apply her lipstick. Impulsively, she stood back, smoothed her dress over her breasts, and viewed herself in profile. Oranges at best, she thought, critically surveying her breasts. Why couldn't she at least have been the size of a decent grapefruit? Underendowed, that's what she was. Her profile image looked back at her and she began to feel ridiculous. And vain. Purposefully, she tried to concentrate on finishing her makeup. Her face was flushed and her eyes were unusually bright. If she didn't know better, she'd say that hers was the look of a woman who had been thoroughly kissed. That was absurd, of course. The kiss had been last night, and Lancelot had nothing whatsoever to do with her sudden attack of vanity. There was something in the air down here.

She was still chiding herself for her foolishness when someone knocked on the door. At least God hadn't made her underendowed and oversexed, she reminded herself. Nothing could be further from her mind than that lobster fisherman. Even if he did have the most wonderful fringe of black eyelashes she had ever seen on a man.

She opened the door and Mark bounced into the room. "Gee, Aunt Alice, you smell good." His innocent remark brought a furious blush to Alice's cheeks. She shoved her glasses firmly up on her nose, stiffened her back, and tried to look as businesslike as possible.

"You're wearing your hair down," Mrs. B said, and beamed at her. "I approve."

Alice thought she might as well hang a sign around her neck that proclaimed her recent, foolish vanity. Still smelling like a gardenia bush, thoroughly flustered, and wondering why she had ever chosen Puerto Vallarta in the first place, she ushered her family to the door. "The taxi's waiting," she said.

Eduardo's villa was sprawled in the foothills of the Sierra Madres, gleaming white amid the lush greenery of trees and the brilliance of jacaranda blossoms. Their host met them at the door, his face shining like polished mahogany and his waxed mustache twirled up at the ends. "Welcome to my home," he greeted them, then led them through a paved courtyard and into a cavernous room. Tables laden with food beckoned the hungry guests. White-coated waiters hovered near the tables, ready to uncover the myriad dishes and uncork the wine.

Alice settled Mark and Mrs. B at a table and then roamed the room on the pretext of seeing that all her crew were properly settled. Lance was late, but the female models she had hired for the evening were standing beneath a massive candelabrum, chatting with Eduardo.

With an expert eye, she assessed the models. They were perfect for tonight's filming. Alice thought their dresses were excessively tight, but that didn't really matter since they would be changing later. She started toward them to introduce herself. Halfway to her destination she heard a commotion at the door and turned to see what had happened.

Lancelot, gorgeous and golden, was walking into the room. A buzz of admiring whispers followed him across the room.

Alice unconsciously smoothed her silk dress over her hips. Maybe she should take off her glasses, she thought. Surreptitiously, she slid them into her purse and again started across the room to greet the models. The furniture, however, had perversely rearranged itself after she'd removed her glasses. "Excuse me," she said to a straight-backed chair. "I beg your pardon," she told a brass urn that threatened to crash to the floor from the impact of her body.

Large hands reached out and grabbed her by the shoulders as she bumped into a solid wall of flesh. Her head jerked up, and even though he was fuzzy around the edges, there was no mistaking Lancelot.

"Somebody must have dimmed the lights," she said. "It's dark in here."

Lancelot chuckled. "Forget your glasses, Alice?"

"No, they're in my purse," she blurted out. Standing this close to him, with his hot hands scalding her flesh, her wits had gone back to Boston and left her floundering around in confusion.

"Allow me." He took her purse and retrieved her glasses. Trying to keep a serious face, he placed them on her nose. "You might miss something." His lips twitched at the corners. The loose hair and the perfume were flirtatious and provocative . . . and as foreign to Alice as blue jeans would be to the queen of England. He was charmed.

"Thank you," she said stiffly. Damn, she berated herself, why did words seem to fail her around this man? Just this once she wanted to be able to make clever small talk. What should she say? Something provocative? Something witty? "How do you like Eduardo's villa?" Oh, great. She sounded like a travelogue.

"I like it much better now that I've seen you in it," he said. He watched the different emotions chase across her face as she struggled with the new role she had unconsciously chosen. An almost forgotten warmth touched the edge of his heart, and he felt a strong need to spare her any embarrassment. He knew that Alice was on safe ground with business. "As a matter of fact," he continued smoothly, "I was looking for you. I thought we might eat dinner together so that I can ask you a few questions about this evening's filming."

Feeling chivalrous but not altogether honest, he steered her to a table in the corner of the vast room. You might as well admit it, he told himself. You enjoyed that kiss every damn bit as much as she did.

Her self-confidence somewhat improved by his matter-of-fact manner, Alice looked at Lance and tried not to think of that golden mat of chest hair hidden under his tuxedo shirt. "We'll use the courtyard for most of the shots, I think. And Eduardo checked the size of the clothes. We shouldn't have the same problems we had yesterday."

"I'm disappointed. I was looking forward to another session with you and the safety pins."

"Mattie will do any necessary alterations tonight," she said stiffly. She lifted her wineglass to her lips and hoped she looked more composed than she felt. By now she knew that Lance was a master of the unexpected comment. Just when she had settled into a relaxed state, he dropped a bomb into the conversation in order to rattle her.

His smile was disarming. "Somehow it won't be the same. Mattie lacks your sensitive touch."

"Don't you ever let up?" she asked, more harshly than she'd intended.

"With what?"

"The teasing. You got me here under the pretext of discussing business, and now you're making me—" She stopped. She couldn't just blurt out that he was making her hot and quivery inside. She stiffened her spine. Small talk, she reminded herself. After all, she was thirty years old. She should be able to handle herself around Lancelot.

He was only her model. "You're making me forget that I'm a lady," she said primly.

He roared with laughter. "You! A lady! If I recall correctly, you can cuss like a sailor, and you don't bat an eyelash at propositioning strange men."

"I generally deal with impertinent remarks by giving the speaker a good clout over the head." Alice tried to keep her face severe, but she was having a hard time holding back the laughter. Lance's sense of humor, however warped it might be, was infectious. She found herself seeing the comedy in situations that would formerly have irritated her.

"Just the way any proper lady would deal with them," he said.

"Precisely."

"I haven't been around proper ladies much over the last few years. Tell me, Alice. How do proper ladies feel about moonlight kisses?"

She hoped he couldn't hear the way her heart thundered at that remark. How proper ladies felt was too steamy to be called proper. "Proper ladies don't discuss things like that in public."

"Do they hold hands in public?" He reached across the table and captured her hand. "Like this?" Lifting the hand to his lips, he planted a slow, moist kiss on her palm. "And this?"

Alice sat so still she could hear the fizz in the champagne two tables away. She decided that before she made a fool of herself and climbed over the tabletop to throw herself into his arms, she had better do something. "Why do you call yourself Lancelot?" she asked softly.

"The name appealed to me at the time. Before that I called myself Galahad." His bluer-than-blue eyes pierced hers, challenging her to search for the man behind the mask.

"Both knights of the Round Table," she said musingly. "You obviously don't go about doing good deeds and rescuing damsels in distress. I could have fallen through the gangplank of that stinking lobster boat without you lifting a finger."

"You're a discerning woman."

Ignoring his last remark, she continued her speculation about his false identity. "Does that mean you're on a quest?" She watched his face change, as if his mask tightened. Putting her finger into the small chink she had found, she continued her line of questioning. "What are you searching for, Galahad-Lancelot?" She felt his hand squeeze hers reflexively. "Are you searching for something you've lost, or for something you never had?"

His eyes became hooded as he withdrew further behind his mask. Abruptly, he released her hand. "I'm afraid I can't claim any such lofty motives. I'm just an ordinary drifter, looking for a warm bed and a warm woman to share it."

Alice knew that his answer was a cover-up, but that didn't bother her the way it should have. She—who had never been content with anything less than a sensible, organized approach to life— found herself accepting Lance on his fantasy credentials without batting an eyelash.

She didn't stop to question her own motives. She would sort them out later. For the moment she would enjoy being near the man who had gallantly rescued her from falling flat on her face. On that count she had been wrong: He *did* rescue damsels in distress.

"I suppose there have been many," she said nonchalantly.

"Many what?"

"Women to warm your bed."

"Yes." His eyes sparkled at her over the rim of his glass. "Are you jealous?"

"Real ladies don't indulge in such useless emotions."

"But then, we both know that you're not a real lady. Don't we, Alice?"

"No, we don't."

"Underneath that ladylike exterior you're hiding a delightful hoyden. And a touch of the cat, I think. A cat that fights and spits and claws and scratches for what it wants."

Alice laughed. "Then I would be careful if I were you." She heard her flippant remark with amazement. If she hadn't known better, she'd say that she was flirting. How had she gone from a woman who barely knew the meaning of the word to one who shamelessly indulged in the frivolous pastime? The golden vagabond fisherman had cast a spell on her, she decided. And it felt so good that she didn't want it to end.

"Why, Miss Alice Spencer, are you flinging down the gauntlet?"

"And if I am?"

"As a seasoned knight of the Round Table, I keep my sword well honed. Be forewarned."

Alice felt giddy and light-headed from too much wine and not enough Lancelot. She would probably wake up tomorrow and find that she had dreamed this entire evening.

"Excuse me, Alice."

She looked up to see Eduardo standing by their table, flanked by the two women models. Thinking of knights with swords and moonlight kisses and gauntlets carelessly flung, she gave Eduardo a dreamy smile. "You have outdone yourself with this delicious banquet, Eduardo."

"Outdone myself?"

"Surpassed all expectations. The food is magnificent," she explained.

His teeth flashed. "I am happy to please you." He beamed at Alice and Lance, enjoying the compliments and almost forgetting why he had come to their table.

"Señor Eduardo." The model with sienna hair prodded his side. "The man."

"Ah, yes." His smile widened. "The models wish to meet the handsome man who will be working with them."

Lancelot rose gracefully to his feet and charmingly introduced himself. Bending his golden head, he brushed his lips fleetingly across the hand of first one model and then the other.

Alice turned green all over. He didn't have to overdo it, she fumed to herself. A nice, sedate handshake would have served the purpose. Or a distant nod. Did he have to fawn over them?

As if he had read her mind, Lance winked at her. She could have died. Was she that transparent? she wondered. She was really batting a thousand tonight—first vanity and now jealousy. Hastily, she tried to make amends. She chatted with the models about tonight's work, trying to make them feel comfortable with the job. The sienna-haired model, Rosalita, spoke very good English, but the other one, Carmen, had a hard time following the conversation. Lance came to her rescue, translating their words into fluent Spanish.

Alice was once again amazed. It wasn't just his command of Spanish. His manner with the models was so relaxed and natural that they were put completely at ease. First Mattie and now this, she thought. Had he abandoned some high-powered public relations job to become a drifter? Captivated by this side of Lance, she sat back in her seat and watched him work his magic.

After Eduardo and the models had left to get ready for the filming, Alice leaned toward Lance. "Thank you for making my job easier. It's very important for my models to be perfectly at ease."

He lifted her hand to his lips. She felt his kiss sizzle all the way down to her toes. "What makes you happy makes me happy."

Thank goodness for gravity, she thought. Otherwise she would have floated right out of her chair. As it was, she remained seated and almost drowned in his electric blue eyes. "I guess . . ." The words died in her throat as a shocking question came to her mind. Was she falling in love with Lancelot? Praying that he couldn't read her thoughts this time, she reached for her water glass. The ice rattled against the sides of the glass as she lifted it to her lips. Shakily, she set it on the table, sloshing water onto the cloth. She cleared her throat and tried again. "It—it's time to start the filming."

Lance looked at the hair falling in soft waves around her flushed face, her slender neck arched gracefully above the high collar of her green dress, and he thought she looked like an exotic flower. He was seized with a sudden, primitive urge to have her. The raw power of the urge shocked him. Dammit, he chided himself, slow down. It was perfectly obvious that Alice was untutored in the ways of love. He would have to romance her, and he was inordinately pleased with the idea. Rising from his chair, he gave her a courtly bow and took her hand. "Allow me, love. Your director's chair awaits."

Alice allowed herself to be led to her chair. Lance and the models disappeared to get ready for the first shot, and it took her several minutes to get his overwhelming golden presence out of her mind. By virtue of strong determination, she finally achieved a semblance of professional detachment, and the session began.

After Lance and the models had been fitted and made up for the last shot, Alice sent a tired Mrs. B back to the hotel with Mattie and Jeanette. Mark begged to stay, so she decided that he could sleep in her room for just this one night. He bounced around happily for all of fifteen minutes after Mrs. B left, and then curled up in a lounge chair and fell asleep.

Finally the shoot was over. "That's a wrap, everybody," Alice announced. "Let's pack up and go home." She sank back into her chair for a moment, limp, then rose to help pack the gear.

She was holding a tripod in her hand when snatches of a conversation between Lance and Rosalita drifted her way. She didn't really mean to eavesdrop, she told herself as she took a few steps backward.

"You don't say," Lance said, his voice sounding intrigued. Overly intrigued, Alice decided. She leaned her head farther back under the pretext of adjusting the end of the tripod. Dammit, she thought. Rosalita was speaking in Spanish.

Lancelot laughed, and the stream of Spanish continued. Alice didn't understand most of the words, but she understood the tone perfectly. The man she liked more than she cared to think about was being propositioned.

"With a water bed and a rose!" Lance's rich laughter exploded behind her.

Alice's back stiffened. A water bed and a rose. Good grief! Forgetting the tripod in her hand, she whirled around. The tripod neatly clipped Rosalita behind the knees, knocking her into the pool. Alice was torn between mortification and laughter.

"I'm so sorry," she said. Struggling to keep a straight face, she leaned over the pool and extended her hand. "Here. Let me help you."

The model called upon every god she knew to rain disaster upon Alice's head. Angrily ignoring the extended hand, she lifted herself from the pool and marched off, her bedraggled skirt trailing behind her on the Spanish tiles.

"Why, Miss Alice Spencer," Lance said. "I'm amazed at your audacity." He chuckled. "You did that on purpose."

Alice smothered her own grin. "Just hush up," she told him tartly. "It's a darn good thing I don't need Miss Overly Endowed for tomorrow's filming." Blissfully ignorant of her slip of the tongue and Lance's smothered guffaw, she went on. "She'll probably never work for me again."

"To say the least," he said, deadpan. He considered it a minor miracle that he managed to speak without cracking up.

"I daresay she'll never speak to me again."

"It's highly probable."

"She might even return with a vigilante group and have me horsewhipped."

"With a knight in shining armor looking on? Tisk, tisk, Miss Alice. Don't you believe in gallantry anymore?"

"Are you gallant, Sir Lancelot?"

"Through and through." He took her elbow and led her across the courtyard. "And to prove my point"—he reached down, lifting Mark into his arms—"I'm going to help you with this sleepy bundle."

After the lively events of the evening, the drive back to the Hotel Camino Real was subdued. Lance and Alice didn't speak, not wanting to wake the sleeping child. The elevator whisked them silently upward, and the thick hall carpet muffled their steps as they walked to Alice's room.

"Where shall I put him?" Lance asked.

She turned back the covers on the bed farthest away from the door and watched as the vagabond fisherman carefully tucked her nephew in. She held her breath as Lance pushed Mark's fair hair back from his forehead and gently pulled the covers over him. He would make a wonderful father, she thought, as he bent down and whispered softly, "Sleep well, little tyke."

The simple domestic picture tugged at her heartstrings, and she was filled with yearning for all that she had missed—the quiet bedtime scenes, the laughter-filled frolicking in a swimming pool, the easy camaraderie between father and son. But most of all she was filled with yearning for this man, this golden drifter, this knight in tarnished armor, this charming wanderer who had come into her life.

Quietly, she slipped onto her balcony and leaned against the railing. With a certainty that needed no rhyme or reason, Alice knew now the answer to her question: She *was* falling in love with Lancelot.

"All finished." He joined her on the small balcony, leaning against the rail beside her. "Beautiful, isn't it?"

"Yes." She lifted her face to the stars. "I could almost stay here forever."

"Forever is a long time, Alice."

She turned so that she could see his profile. There was a faraway look in his eyes as he gazed out across Banderas Bay. A small fear squeezed her heart as she thought of the sorrow of being in love with a wayfaring man. But it was already too late. She could no more stop her feelings than she could stop the sun from rising in the east.

Six

Lance turned to face her in the moonlight. "Do you like to dance, love?"

His deep, rich voice wrapped around her in quiet seduction as he asked the unexpected question. "Why, yes. But it's been—" She bit off the word *years*. There was no need to confess her bereft social life to him. "A long time," she finished.

"We're going tonight."

"What?"

"I said . . ."

"I know what you said. I can't go dancing. Mark is in my room and Mrs. B is fast asleep and it's late . . ." She stopped for a gulping breath. Dancing in his arms would be heaven, she thought. ". . . and I hadn't planned to go . . ." Her words trailed off as he lifted her hair and planted a soft kiss at the nape of her neck.

". . . dancing," she sighed.

"Sometimes those things we don't plan are the most fun." He smiled down at her. "We'll leave as soon as the baby-sitter gets here."

"You called a baby-sitter?" She meant for her words to be an accusation, a recrimination for his high-handed methods, but they came out dreamy. Going dancing with Lancelot was just about the most romantic thing she could possibly imagine.

"From Eduardo's," he said. "After Mrs. B left. Eduardo recommended this young man, and I liked the way he sounded on the phone. He's taken a year off from college so that he can earn enough money to go back next year."

"You did all that without asking me?" She asked the question just to preserve appearances. She would never dream of turning him down. Why, if he had said they were going on a rocket ship to the moon, she would have gone out and bought a space suit.

"When I make up my mind that I want something I go after it."

She trembled at his words. His face was carved into determined lines, and she heard the cavalry charge in his voice. Was she the something he wanted, or was it just the dancing? she wondered.

The baby-sitter arrived and Alice, who was accustomed to taking complete charge of Mark, contentedly watched as Lance gave the young man lengthy instructions. She supposed that Lance's authoritative manner and his supreme self-confidence elicited the trust she felt.

Alice understood only snatches of the Spanish, but she thought she heard Lance mention scholarships and jobs. What was he up to now? The more she learned about the man, the more intrigued she became.

In the elevator, she turned to him. "Did I hear you offer Carlos a scholarship and a job?"

He laughed. "I thought you didn't speak Spanish."

"Two years of high-school Spanish from a teacher who would make Hitler look like a pussycat furthered my education in that area. You didn't answer my question."

He took her arm and escorted her to a waiting taxi. "I did."

"How could you do that?" she asked with feigned innocence as she stepped into the cab. "And you a mere lobster fisherman?"

He settled beside her on the seat, then leaned over and nibbled her ear. "You shouldn't go fishing alone. You might get into water over your head." He arranged her head on his shoulder and amazed himself by thinking how good it felt. Just this small physical contact stirred such a warmth and protectiveness in him. If he were given to poetic turns of phrase, he would say that his heart was thawing. He smiled wryly.

At first Alice held herself stiffly against his side, then she began to relax and enjoy the new sensations that were sweeping through her. She was tinglingly aware of his body touching hers, especially the muscled thigh pressing against her silk-clad leg. A strange heat settled in her groin. She felt languorous and contented. Was love supposed to feel this way?

She nestled her head closer against his shoulder. "I'm not afraid of getting into water over my head. How could you offer Carlos a scholarship and a job?"

"Family connections." His hand caressed her upper arm. Always the courageous Alice Spencer, he thought. Proclaiming fearlessness of water when she couldn't even swim. He certainly planned to take her into water over her head. He only hoped that he could do it with a skill and expertise that would make the initiation wonderful for her.

He had chosen an informal club with a large, open courtyard and strolling musicians. At their table he startled Alice by pulling his chair close to hers and draping his arm casually across her shoulders. "Cozier, don't you think?"

She was beyond thinking. With candlelight casting a romantic spell and the stars spread in a shining canopy overhead, she was transported to a fantasy world, one she had never visited before. Surreptitiously, she pinched herself to see if it were really she sitting beside this handsome man in this glorious setting.

Lance ordered her a mysterious purple drink that she wouldn't have dared touch under ordinary circumstances. She could practically see exotic potions fizzing in its frothy depths. The circumstances were extraordinary, however, and the man beside her was pure magic. She closed her eyes and took a tentative sip.

"Do you always drink with your eyes squinched up like that?" he asked teasingly.

"Sometimes it helps not to see what you're doing." The purple drink burned her throat and settled like a ball of fire in the pit of her stomach. "What is this stuff?"

"Attitude adjuster."

"I'm not sure I can trust a man who orders a drink like this."

"I'm not sure you can either." He rose and pulled her from her chair. "They're playing our song."

Alice loved dancing, and she swung easily into the slow rhythm of the music.

"You're too far away, love." Lance's arm tightened across her back, bringing her shockingly close to his hard body.

She sucked in her breath and missed a beat as she felt the full length of him through her silk dress. My goodness, what was happening to her? she wondered wildly. Her legs felt limp and useless, and that bold maleness against her thighs excited her imagination to a fever pitch. Was she expected to *dance* like this? On rubber legs and with that . . . Oh my, what was she supposed to do next? Was she being compromised? Seduced? Was there such a thing as making love on the dance floor? She thought so. She tried to back away from the disturbing closeness. It was all too new to her.

"You dance well, Alice," he murmured. Smiling down at her, he tightened his hold so that no more than a hairbreadth of space separated them.

"So do you," she said lamely. She marveled that she was actually able to speak.

Loving the feel of her and enjoying the process of initiating her to a man's touch, Lance kept her on the dance floor through four consecutive songs, all of them dreamy ballads. He didn't question his own motives. He wasn't ready to indulge in that kind of soul-searching. He only knew that he was determined to have Alice Spencer.

When he finally escorted her back to their table Alice had mixed feelings of relief and regret. Perhaps if she had been in Boston, she could have handled the situation better. But she was under the spell of Puerto Vallarta and a certain vagabond fisherman. She would enjoy what was happening to her and think about it another day.

Maybe the purple drinks were at fault. She had two. Or perhaps the music and the stars could be blamed. Whatever it was, she thought Lancelot was the most fascinating, most intelligent man she had ever met. They talked about books and music and politics. They discussed travel and theater and science. And they danced.

When they went back to the Hotel Camino Real the morning sun was beginning to pink the eastern sky. Alice had never known a night to fly by so quickly. At her door, Lance gathered her into his arms. "Tonight the stars, tomorrow the moon," he said. He kissed her thoroughly and pushed her gently through the door. "I'll see you at the crack of noon, my sweet."

She fell into an exhausted sleep and dreamed of a golden knight on a white charger and of the reluctant, laughing maiden, whom he carried to a lush green meadow. Alice was awakened by Mark before she could find out what happened to the maiden.

Mark sat on her bed, talking excitedly about the shooting the night before and what he and Mrs. B had planned to do that day. Alice guiltily smothered one yawn after another as she listened, until Mrs. B arrived a few minutes later. Alice waved good-bye as the two of them left, then fell immediately back to sleep.

When she opened her eyes again, feeling fully rested, she saw that the sun was pouring through her window. Raising her arms above her head, she stretched luxuriously. She was in a carnival mood. There would be no filming today, and last night she had promised to spend the day with Lancelot. She dressed quickly in walking shorts and a cotton camp shirt, and was waiting breathlessly beside the door when he knocked.

"Hi!" she said cheerfully.

Lance looked at her sparkling eyes and flushed face, and hoped he didn't botch things by pushing her too fast. He knew that a slow seduction was required, and he vowed to temper his own eagerness with caution. "Hi, yourself. Ready?"

"Yes. Mrs. B came earlier to get Mark. They're spending the day on the beach."

"We are too. At least, some part of the day. Grab a sweater. It gets chilly on the water at night."

Alice obeyed without question. It didn't matter to her where they went as long as they were together. They wandered through quaint little back streets and plundered interesting shops. They found a bookstore that specialized in old books, and both of them were soon up to their elbows in dusty, yellowing editions.

"I could spend days in here," Alice said, looking up from the book she was holding. "Books were my world when I was a child."

Lance gave her a dazzling smile. "There's dust on your nose," he said. He cupped his hand under her chin and rubbed the spot with his thumb.

"Thanks," she said breathlessly. Funny what such a simple gesture did to her, she mused. Her heart was beating so hard, she was certain he could hear. She lowered her gaze to the book in her hand.

"You're welcome." With his hand still lingering on her face, he brushed a butterfly kiss against her cheek.

Her face burned from his touch, and she hastily turned back to the bookshelf. Lord, was she allowed to feel like this in a public place? she wondered. All dreamy inside and slightly wicked? Oh dear! And it felt so wonderful she wouldn't have cared if he had kissed her in the middle of the most proper restaurant in Boston.

"Alice!" Lance suddenly exclaimed. "Would you

look at this?" He showed her a dog-eared edition of *Typee*. "What do you think?"

She took the book carefully and inspected it. "It's impossible to tell for sure with these nineteenth-century books, but I think it's a first edition." She handed the book back to Lance. "Do you like Melville?"

"Yes. He's a man after my own heart."

She laughed. "He would be. What an adventurer he was!"

Lance paid a princely sum for the book, then escorted Alice out into the sunshine. "For you," he said. He placed the book in her hands and kissed her on the tip of the nose.

"I can't possibly accept such an expensive gift."

"You can't possibly refuse." He closed her hands firmly around the book and smiled at her.

"Oh, Lance!" she breathed. "Thank you." What was the meaning of this? Kisses in public. Expensive gifts. "But why?"

He laughed. "Spoken like the Miss Alice Spencer I know. Where are your Southern manners, woman? You're supposed to bat your eyelashes and say, 'For little ol' me?' " He pulled her into his arms so that a large crowd of tourists could get by. His lips were so close to hers that, for a moment, she thought he was going to kiss her again. Holding her with the mesmerizing power of his blue eyes, he seduced her with his rich baritone drawl. "*Typee* reminds me of how marvelous it would be to be stranded on a desert island . . . with you. It's a memorable gift for a memorable day."

It was remarkable that she could speak, considering that she had floated off into the clouds. "Has the day been memorable?" she whispered.

"Yes. And it's going to become even more so."

Hugging his words and her precious package next to her heart, she strolled down the street with her golden knight. The more she learned about him, the less tarnished his armor became. He caught her sideways look and winked. He didn't know just how memorable the day was, she thought. It was the day that she fell hopelessly in love.

They stopped at a small sidewalk café. Feeling adventurous and giddy and not quite herself, Alice brushed the menu aside. "I think I'll see just how much Spanish old Hitler taught me," she explained. Boldly, she placed her order.

The waiter scratched his head in puzzlement, and Lance burst into laughter. "You just ordered fried shoes."

Alice joined in his laughter. "I'm fond of soft leather, but not that fond. Go ahead and order for me."

"What would you like?"

"Anything. As long as it's not *zapatos*."

"I love a woman who can laugh at herself."

Alice beamed. While he hadn't actually said that he loved her, it was close enough. With just a little fantasizing she could pretend that they were two people madly in love, exploring the romantic city together. After they ate they searched the city for old Spanish cathedrals. Both were history buffs, and both loved the grand architecture of the ancient buildings.

The setting sun was painting the city with rainbow hues of pink and purple when they emerged from the last cathedral. Lance bought some tacos from a street vendor and hailed a cab.

"Where are we going?" Alice asked as they

passed the public part of the beach and turned onto a dusty, seemingly seldom traveled road.

"You'll see."

The cab stopped in a secluded area screened by palmetto trees and rampant with jacaranda blossoms.

"Lance, this place is deserted."

"Exactly." He helped her from the cab, had a lengthy conversation with the driver, and pulled his packages from the trunk.

As the cab drove off in a cloud of dust, Lance took a gaily striped, handwoven blanket from one of his packages and spread it on the ground. "Picnic by the sea." He winked at her.

"So that's why you bought the blanket." She shivered, partly from the cool breeze coming off the water, but mostly from thinking of being on that blanket in this deserted spot with Lancelot.

"I always plan ahead." He put his arm around her and drew her down. "Cold, love?"

"I'll put on my sweater," she mumbled. Chiding herself for being so foolishly afraid, she pulled her sweater about her shoulders. What did she think he was going to do? Ravish her? Her mouth went dry and she shivered again. She was even more scandalized by the realization that she wished he would. She folded her hands primly in her lap and lowered her eyes. Well, maybe not ravish her, but at least kiss her shamelessly.

Lance hid his smile as he unwrapped the still hot tacos and uncorked a bottle of wine. Dear proper Alice, he thought. Such a pity that all her warmth and sensuality had been locked inside her for so many years. And she was a sensual woman. Her charm lay in the fact that she didn't know it. Certain mannerisms—a provocative tilt of the head, an unconsciously flirtatious glance from under lowered lashes, a deep-throated, sexy laugh—had beguiled him all day long. He was eager to see if the time was right for the liberation of Miss Alice Spencer. He poured the wine into paper cups and didn't stop to ponder his own eagerness.

Alice took the cup he offered her and raised it to her lips. "At least it's not purple," she said wryly.

His eyes sparkled with suppressed mirth. "I'm not sure you can trust a man who plies you with wine either, Miss Spencer."

"I'm equal to the occasion, Sir Lancelot. Pass the tacos." She hoped her brave words would be a proper shield for the advances she half desired and half dreaded.

She was granted a reprieve as they ate. They watched the sun set over the bay, and Lance talked of inconsequential things—other sunsets he had seen, other tacos he had eaten. Alice wondered if he were softening her up for the kill.

After they had eaten he put the paper cups and taco wrappers into an empty bag and stretched out on the blanket. He cradled his head on his arms and looked up at her with innocent blue eyes. "It's comfortable down here. Why don't you join me?"

Her spine stiffened and goose bumps popped up on her arms. "I'm fine up here. Thank you."

He smiled. "Do you see that bird flying by?"

"What bird?" She tilted her head upward.

"Not over there." He pointed to the palmetto trees on the other side of his broad chest. "Over here."

As she leaned down to follow his pointing finger, he reached up and captured her lips. "You lied," she murmured against his mouth.

"So I did."

"You're . . . an . . . untrustworthy . . . rogue," she whispered breathlessly between his nibbling kisses.

"Indeed, I am." His arm encircled her waist and he pulled her down beside him. "Comfortable?"

She held herself ramrod straight, trying to put as much space as she could between her and that magnificently muscled, completely relaxed male body. "Yes," she lied.

"Here. Let me massage your neck." He lifted himself on one elbow and began a slow, sensuous caressing with his hands. "Just relax, Alice. This won't hurt a bit."

Her eyes widened and she made a strangled sound that masqueraded as a word. Oh Lord, what were his fingers doing on the back of her neck, and why did they feel so good? Against her will, her body began to go limp. First her traitorous legs melted against his, and then her torso molded itself to his magnificent chest.

In slow motion he lowered his head and with his lips traced a burning path down the side of her neck. He found the hollow at the base of her throat and stopped to feast on the soft, pulsing skin.

Alice closed her eyes as astonishing sensations assaulted her. Tentatively, she lifted her hands and touched his hair. It felt like silk, and she thought she would remember its texture for the rest of her life. Burying her hands in the soft hair, she unconsciously pulled his head closer.

His lips moved upward and descended hungrily on hers. Moaning low in his throat, he nestled her body against his. His hands moved possessively along her back, caressing her tense muscles. "Relax, love, relax," he murmured.

The kisses were magic, she thought. Heaven.

But what were his hands doing now? They had pulled her shirt from the waistband of her shorts and were boldly touching her naked flesh. She stiffened reflexively and the movement thrust her hips against his. Panic seized her as she felt the evidence of his desire. "No," she whispered raggedly.

"I want you, my darling." The hands moved seductively on her back.

"I . . . I can't.

"Dare, my darling. Dare," he urged, his mouth still against hers.

"No." Her voice was a forlorn whisper as she silently cursed the coward inside who wouldn't risk her heart on a dare. The golden man was hers for the taking and she was afraid.

Relief flooded her as she felt his hands tuck her shirt back in. His kiss softened to a gentle touching, and finally he lifted his head and cradled her in his arms. "Look at the stars, love," he said gently. "I think I see Orion."

She gazed up at the stars without seeing them. What had stopped her? she wondered. Did she want commitment? She had known he was a loner before she kissed him. Men like Lance didn't make commitments. Heaven knows, he had said it often enough. What then? Why hadn't she taken the pleasure he offered her? Wasn't that what she wanted?

Alice sighed. She didn't know. Since Lance had come into her life there were lots of things she didn't know anymore. Was love always this puzzling? She wanted him so much she ached just thinking about it, and yet she was afraid to reach out, afraid of being hurt. Dare, he had said to her, dare. Did she dare give herself to this man, this vagabond who would never return her committed love?

Not yet. She just couldn't. Listening to the musical cadence of his voice as he pointed out the constellations, she gradually relaxed. She could even think about her missed opportunity with wry humor. All in all, she decided, it was just as well she hadn't succumbed to temptation. Women bent on seduction didn't wear sensible cotton panties.

Skilled in the ways of women, Lancelot knew he had to back off and give Alice some space. She needed time to think about everything that was happening to her.

During the rest of the filming in Puerto Vallarta, he behaved like an angel. He was cooperative and charming in a distant sort of way. Alice was vaguely disappointed. There were no repeat kisses in the moonlight, no more heated embraces by the sea. The filming went like clockwork, and the commercials were wrapped up two days ahead of schedule.

Mrs. B and Mark returned to Boston the next day, and Alice called her assistant. "Tom," she said, "I want you to meet Mrs. B and Mark at the airport."

"I'll be glad to, Alice. When does their flight come in?" Even across the miles Tom's voice boomed with good cheer.

She gave him the flight information, then asked about business. The question was unnecessary, she knew. Tom was remarkably efficient and thorough. He gave her a glowing report and then inquired about her job in Puerto Vallarta.

"We're finished here. We're having problems

with the connector cables on one of the cameras, though. Alex is going to call you about having some shipped down. In the meantime, I'll leave for the Yucatán to set up camp so that we can start filming as soon as the crew can follow me."

"Dammit, Alice. Don't you go down there by yourself," Tom bellowed over the phone.

Alice rolled her eyes at his brotherly protection of her. "I didn't say that."

"You didn't have to say it. I know you. The jungle is no place for a woman alone. Take one of the crew."

"I'm planning to," she said meekly. But the sparkle in her eyes was not meek at all.

"Alice, I know that tone of voice. Hell, you'd jump into a pit of snakes if you thought it would be good for the business. I'm going to tell Alex to send somebody with you. To personally make sure you don't go by yourself."

"You worry too much. Tell Kathy and the children I said hello."

Alice looked at her seat companion on the plane and her mouth went dry. She didn't know whether to thank Alex or kill him for sending Lance along with her. The rest of the crew had opted to stay behind in Puerto Vallarta until the camera was in operation again. As Alex had explained to Alice, they didn't want to leave civilization for a steamy jungle until they had to. He had also insisted on sending someone ahead with her—one of the crew, he had said. Some crew, Alice thought, as she boldly studied the sleeping Lancelot. Could she survive two days in the jungle with him without throwing herself at his feet? Probably not.

How was it possible, she wondered, for her to love him so intensely and for him to be totally oblivious to that love? And she did love him. Completely and without question. She had hardly slept a wink since their picnic on the beach. Why, why had she turned him down? The man who laughed easily and quickly, and who did wonderful, impulsive things, such as presenting her with a rare book and arranging a picnic for them under the stars. There would never be another missed opportunity, she vowed. She was ready to risk her heart on a dare.

His eyes suddenly popped open. "A penny for your thoughts," he said.

"You weren't asleep," she accused.

"No. I was watching you."

"How could you? Your eyes were closed."

"Looks can be deceiving."

"Why are you here?"

"It's the only way I can get to the Yucatán."

"You know what I mean."

"Cheer up, Alice." He chucked her playfully under the chin. "I might come in handy. I used to be a boy scout."

"When you were growing up in South Carolina?" Alice baited the hook and dropped it casually in front of him.

He didn't bite. Leaning across her, he glanced out the window. "We're coming in for a landing."

The jet's tires squealed on the runway as it touched down in Mérida. Alice and Lance directed the loading of a bus that would take them a hundred miles inland. Magnificent sixteenth-century Spanish cathedrals gave way to henequen farms and cattle lands, which were rapidly replaced by the dense growth of the tropical jungle as the ancient bus chugged inland.

Conversation was sparse on the bus ride as each of them soaked up the scenery and concentrated on private thoughts. Alice's thoughts raced, squirrellike, in her head. *Two* days, at least two days, alone with Lancelot. Separate tents? Would he or wouldn't he? Would *she*? Yes, yes, *yes*. But what if he didn't ask? She'd kill him. Didn't he *know* she loved him?

Lance's thoughts were more introspective. He wanted Alice. There was no doubt about it. But was she ready? It was hard to tell. Was *he* ready? She wasn't the ships-passing-in-the-night kind of woman who would hand him his hat and send him on his merry way. Was his way merry anymore? Or was it beginning to go a little stale? Dammit, he wasn't ready for commitment. He didn't want to hurt Alice, but . . . Damn!

The 1950s bus deposited them in the jungle and headed back to Mérida. Alice looked at the masses of equipment and supplies that had to be transformed into a campsite. Suddenly she was very glad to have Lance along for more reasons than those of deep and wild attraction.

"You set up the tents while I sort through the cooking gear," she directed him.

"I don't do tents."

"I thought you were a boy scout."

"I was." He grinned at her. "I didn't advance as far as tents."

"Hell. A lot of help you're going to be." She jerked the canvas and poles from the carrying bag.

"Ladies don't cuss."

"Dammit. I'm not a lady." She shoved her glasses

firmly up her nose and scrambled around in the bag.

"That makes everything so much easier." He began clearing a space on the jungle floor for the small hibachi grill. Glancing up from his task, he asked, "What are you looking for?"

"Instructions. Don't these things come with instructions?"

"Just stick the poles in the ground and stretch the canvas over them."

"If you know all that, why aren't you setting up the tent instead of playing tiddleywinks on the ground?"

He stiffened his back in pretended offense. "I'll have you know, ma'am, that I am engaged in a complicated engineering task whose end result will be food for the hungry."

"Then hurry. I'm starved." She looked back from Lance to the tent in her hand. "Eureka!" she shouted. She had suddenly realized that she was holding a simple pup tent, the kind she had seen on *Mister Rogers' Neighborhood* with Mark. One small maneuver and the tent would pop right up. She tried one small maneuver. And then two. And then three. None of them worked.

"Like this." Lance took the tent from her hands and popped it open with no effort at all.

"I thought you didn't do tents," she snapped.

"I lied." His disarming smile defused her anger and made her knees go weak.

"You seem to do a lot of that," she said.

"I consider it an art."

"You could give lessons."

"Speaking of lessons . . . That looks mighty like a swimming hole over there. How about a swimming lesson?" He indicated a small stream that meandered through the jungle beside their campsite.

Smiling at his unique Southern phrasing, she glanced from Lance to the water and back again. "No thanks."

"Everybody should know how to swim."

"Who made you an expert on what everybody should do?"

"Self-appointed."

"Arrogant," she countered.

"Guilty." He smiled, then suddenly turned serious. "Why are you afraid of the water?"

His abrupt question caught her off guard and she answered without thinking. "Heather drowned. I was never the athletic type anyway, and after her death I had nightmares about the water." Because she was a very private person Alice had never before discussed her fear of the water. Somehow the confession felt right with Lance, and she suspected that her heady attraction to him and newfound love made her vulnerable. Laughing to dispel the somberness, she added, "I don't mind getting my feet wet, but I don't want my face in the water. Are we going to stand here all day and discuss my phobias, or are we going to eat?"

"I can see I'm stranded in the jungle with a bossy woman."

"Right. And if you don't like it, you can flag the next bus to town."

"As I recall, the next bus to town comes by in about two days." With the deftness of a seasoned camper, he heated a can of pork and beans over the glowing coals he had been preparing for the grill. Watching Alice return to the unpacking, he divided the food onto two tin plates. He was amazed at how relaxed she was out here in the jungle, at how easily she joined into his light banter. She almost made him believe that she was accustomed to these exchanged with men. But he knew better. He remembered her trembling hands as she had fitted his pants, her hesitant response to his kiss beside the pool, and the way she had become breathless at the idea of making love. Alice had never been with a man . . . and there was his dilemma. The first time for a woman was special. Could he be that first lover and then walk away, turn his back on her and continue his vagabond way of life?

His voice reflected his strain as he called, "Lunch is served."

She looked up from the bundles she was unpacking. Her usually neat clothing was askew, and strands of rich brown hair had slipped from her topknot. The sun, slanting through the canopy of jungle trees, dappled her with gold. Behind her glasses, her eyes were sparkling with a radiance that once again reminded Lance of the Mediterranean. She was fresh and heart-tuggingly appealing.

"Damn," he muttered softly.

Carrying a ground cloth in her hand, she walked over to him. She shook the cloth open and spread it neatly on the ground. In the same proper manner she would have used at Locke-Ober, she sat on the cloth and smiled at Lance. "Did you say something?"

"Lunch is ready."

"No. After that."

"I was just clearing my throat." He handed her a plate. "Do you want Chablis or rosé with your filet mignon?" He held up two cans of soda, orange and cola.

Alice laughed. She was feeling giddy again and carefree, and she wondered when Lance would kiss her. After all, they were completely cut off from civilization, just the two of them alone in the jungle. What more could a man ask? It was the perfect setting for a seduction. So why didn't he start seducing? Couldn't he tell she was ready?

"Make mine Chablis." She took the drink from him, and their fingers made contact on the can. They both froze for a second as the accidental touch sent an electric current bolting through them.

Lance was the first to move his hand. Feigning nonchalance he asked, "How's the steak, Alice?"

How could he be so cool when she was burning up inside? she wondered. Her disappointment showed in her voice. "Mine's tough."

Lance had hoped anger would be her reaction to his nonchalance. Better that she be angry than scared to death, he thought. If she knew what a hard time he was having keeping his hands off her, she would probably be trying to hike all the way back to Puerto Vallarta.

They ate in silence. When he was through Lance stood up, yawning. "I think I'll swing the hammock between those two trees over there and take a siesta."

"How Spanish of you," she said tartly. She jumped up and folded the ground cloth with unnecessary vigor. If he thought she was going to grovel at his feet like most women, he was sadly mistaken, she told herself. She had managed for thirty years without a man. Two more days wouldn't kill her.

"You might be content to while your life away doing nothing. I'm not." She slammed the cloth into a bag and shoved the bag into the tent. "I'm going to scout locations."

"Don't let the snakes bite," he called over his shoulder as he sauntered toward the trees.

"They wouldn't dare!" Holding her head high and her back stiff, Alice marched off. If he laughed, she'd bop him over the head with the hibachi. He did, but she didn't.

Seven

Still fuming, Alice walked along the side of the stream, being careful not to lose sight of the camp. There were dozens of breathtaking settings for the commercials she had in mind. If she hadn't been so overwrought by Lance's rejection, she would have been delighted by the prospect of using these gorgeous backdrops for the commercials.

Low hanging branches snatched at her topknot, pulling most of the hair loose. She finally removed the hairpins and stuck them in her pants' pocket. It was useless to argue with a jungle tree. Anyhow, who cared how her hair looked out here? Certainly Lance didn't. For all his interest since their picnic, she might as well have been a piece of furniture. Or a rock. Or a bespectacled old frump.

She clenched her fists at her sides as she turned back toward the camp. She was *not* a sexless frump. Maybe she wore glasses and didn't have breasts that had to be carried around in a wheel-barrow, but she had feelings and longings and . . . and passion. Yes, passion. Over the last few days she had discovered a deep reservoir of passion within herself, pushing against its walls, straining to be turned loose.

As she neared the camp she looked at Lance, asleep on the hammock. Oh, dammit, she moaned to herself. Why didn't he know? Nobody else could satisfy her longings. Nobody else could release her pent-up desire. Nobody would do except the vagabond fisherman. He was everything she wanted, everything she needed. He was her knight in tarnished armor, her hero with clay feet. He was her love.

The intensity of her feelings shook Alice to the core. Looking frantically around for an escape from the demons that pursued her, she spotted a tropical paradise on the far side of the stream. Quickly, she assessed the water. It was clear and shallow. Without hesitation, she pulled off her shoes, rolled up her pants, and waded in. Damn the torpedoes and full speed ahead, she thought.

She hadn't gone far when she heard Lance's amused voice. "Going wading?"

She turned. He was standing on the bank, watching her. She thought he looked like a golden lion with the lush jungle behind him. He was so impossibly handsome that her heart wrenched just looking at him. She was filled with such an ache that tears of frustration sprang to her eyes. Dammit, she thought, if he couldn't love her why didn't he just leave her alone? "Don't let me disturb your nap," she said. "Go back to your hammock."

"I have a better idea." He stepped into the water. "Why don't I join you?"

Alice was in no mood for his teasing. Her hair had been snatched down by brambles, the steamy tropical heat had wilted her blouse, and on top of all that she was standing on a pointed rock that made her foot hurt. Swiftly, she bent down and picked up the rock. "Stay away from me, Lance." She held the dripping weapon aloft.

"Don't you like me anymore, Alice?" he asked softly, still walking toward her.

"Go back to your hammock and leave me alone, you scoundrel." She knew that she was being irrational, but she didn't care. Here they were in paradise, and for all he noticed it might as well have been New Jersey. She took a step backward, directly into a hole. She lost her balance and fell into the water.

She came up sputtering and gasping for breath. The water at that particular spot was deep enough to scare her. Her hands were shaking as she slipped her glasses off and brushed her wet hair out of her eyes.

Lance scooped her out of the water and hugged her to his chest. "Are you all right?"

Still shaken, she nodded her head.

"Let's get you out of those wet clothes," he said gently as he carried her back to the camp.

Her fright was short-lived as she became aware of his touch. She could feel the heat of his hands through her soggy blouse, and she wanted to stay in his arms forever. The thought made her tremble.

He tightened his hold on her. "It's all right, love. I'll have you fixed up in no time at all."

She smiled. Why, he was coddling her just like a child, she thought. What would he do if he knew why she had trembled? Would he quench the fires that were burning inside her, the flames he had kindled on the beach?

He deposited her tenderly beside the small tent.

"Get into some dry clothes," he said gruffly. Lord, if she only knew how close he had come to losing control back there in the stream! he thought. He spun on his heel and walked a short distance into the jungle. Prowling about, he sought relief from the demons of desire that pursued him. He must not take her carelessly. She was more than an object of passion: she was a vibrant woman with a courageous, questing spirit. He wanted the first time for her to be a pleasuring of the mind as well as a pleasuring of the body. Damn! Was he equal to the challenge?

Alice's hands shook as she removed her dripping clothes. She had felt almost naked in Lance's arms as he had carried her from the stream. A helpless longing welled up in her, and she knotted her fists in frustration. All those years! All those wasted years when she had been wrong. She was not Heather, whose featherbrain had led her indiscriminately into the arms of whatever man was available at the time. She was sane, sensible Alice. And she had chosen her man, a man of fire and spirit, of tender sweetness. She knew, as surely as the sun knows its appointed time to rise, that she could entrust herself to him. Perhaps he would never commit himself to her, but he would never, never hurt her. She was smiling as she left the tent.

From across the clearing Lancelot answered her smile. "All dry now?"

"Yes." With quiet dignity she moved toward him. "Except for my hair." She pulled the towel from around her head and shook her wet hair. "I'm afraid it's hopeless."

"Let me. I'm the next best thing to a hair dryer."

She relinquished her towel to him and almost

drowned in the electric blue of his eyes as she looked up at him.

He bowed gallantly from the waist, then swung his arm to indicate a blanket spread in a jungle bower. "Come into my parlor."

" 'Said the spider to the fly'?" Her breath caught in her throat as she lowered herself to the blanket. The sweet spicy smell of jacaranda blossoms surrounded her.

"Wrong." He sat down beside her, took her glasses off and carefully set them aside, then began to slowly, tenderly towel dry her hair. "Said a knight in shining armor to his lady fair."

Little tingles of fire coursed through her veins as she submitted to the hair-drying. If the beauty salons only knew what an improvement this method was over the impersonal whirring inside those hideous plastic hoods, she thought, they'd be clamoring for Lancelot's services. Her lips curved upward in an impish smile.

"Bend your head forward, love."

She did as she was told, and felt the rough texture of the towel against the nape of her neck. His hands guided the towel in circular motions, slower and slower, until the motions became erotic. A disturbing heat started in her cheeks and spread its warmth through her body.

With her head bowed and the soft, vulnerable skin underneath her hair exposed, Lance thought that Alice looked like a fragile, trusting bird. The towel slid from his hands as he bent to plant a brief kiss on the nape of her arched neck. "All finished, love." *Oh, Lord,* he silently prayed, *don't let me hurt her.*

She lifted her head and smiled at him. She reflected that she might never have another chance like this to tell Lance how she felt. She wanted to thank him for the magic of Puerto Vallarta. She wanted to tell him that she trusted him. But most of all, she wanted to wrap him in her arms and tell him that he always had a home in her heart.

"Thank you," she said softly, and then she could say no more. Years of practiced constraint stopped her.

He saw the struggle in her eyes, and a slow joy spread through his body. He had come to know her so well! He could almost see the walls of her reserve come tumbling down. She was ready to explore the wonderful possibilities of being a woman, and he would show her the way.

He plucked a brilliant jacaranda blossom and tucked it behind her ear. "Lovely Alice, my shy little bird," he murmured as his lips sought hers. With infinite care, he began the ancient ritual of love.

Alice welcomed the familiar sweetness of his mouth. In her jungle bower, redolent with exotic blossoms and echoing with distant birdcalls, she gave herself up to the magic that stole over her.

His arms tightened around her as he deepened the kiss. Using the tip of his tongue, he teased her lips until they flowered open for him. She gave a strangled cry as his tongue plunged inside to take the honeyed sweetness of her mouth.

He lifted his head. "Alice?"

"Please, Lance." Her breath came in ragged spurts. "Please don't stop."

His tongue entered her mouth once more, and he coaxed hers into an erotic duel, a prelude to love. Her senses were drugged as the delicious movement inside her mouth became bolder and stronger. She wove her hands into his hair and pulled his head closer. Primitive emotions that she had not known she possessed burst their bonds and spilled over, sending a wave of desire rushing through her body.

Lance lifted his head and gazed into her unnaturally bright eyes. Her vulnerability shook him to the core. He saw desire shining nakedly in her eyes, but he also saw fear. "I want to share the wonder that can happen between a man and a woman," he said softly. His hands pushed her soft hair back from her forehead. "I have to be very sure that it's what you want too."

The steady strength of his hands on her face reassured her. "I couldn't bear it if you left me now," she whispered.

He kissed the pulse point of her throat as his hands tenderly caressed her breasts through her light cotton shirt. Astonishing sensations swept through Alice, and she trembled as she edged closer to the brink of the unknown. Lance's hands hovered over the buttons of her shirt. "Alice?"

"Yes," she whispered. "Oh, yes." Her words disappeared on a soft sigh.

With gentle care, he undid the top button. "You're sure?" he asked hoarsely. Even now, with things having come so far, he knew that he could stop. Soon, very soon, there would be no turning back.

"Please, Lance." Her eyes were lambent with passion as she looked up at him. "I've wanted you for so long. So very long." She sighed as his lips traced the path of his hands down the open front of her blouse.

Dimly, she felt the fabric flutter to the ground. In a hot haze, she was aware of his expert fingers on the hooks of her bra. Freed at last, her small breasts knew the magic of a man's tongue. She moaned softly as he teased and suckled her breasts until they were peaked, hardened cores of desire. Fire coursed rapidly along her veins, and she went limp in his arms.

Gently, Lance lowered her to the blanket, then shed his own clothing. Alice looked up at him with pure adoration. His eyes were fiery blue diamonds in a carved, golden face. She wanted to memorize this moment, to hold it next to her heart forever.

"I won't hurt you, darling." His husky voice wrapped her in velvet as he lowered his head to her breasts. "I promise," he whispered, and his long, hard body settled against hers.

Involuntarily, she flinched at the first contact of his naked flesh. Her eyes went wide as she felt the powerful evidence of his desire pushing against her thigh.

"It will be all right, Alice," he murmured as his hands traveled soothingly down the slope of her waist and across the curve of her hips. "Trust me."

His touch caused a molten warmth between her thighs and a peculiar tightening of her breasts. "I do," she whispered. The tension gradually flowed out of her as his hands continued their gentling, and she gave herself up to the sweet yearnings of her body.

Lance's lips burned across the delicate arch of her neck and began a tantalizing journey downward. They seemed to be having a delicious feast, tasting, nibbling small bits of her body until she was totally consumed by him. Stunned by the sensations that were overpowering her, she relinquished the last of her inhibitions, forgetting everything except the golden man beside her and the magic of the moment.

Timidly, at first, her body began to move under his searching lips. Then, as the embers inside her were fanned into flames, her movements became bolder. She writhed beneath him, wild with wanting. "Please, Lance," she begged.

"Soon, love. Soon." He lifted his head and rose up on one elbow. "Alice," he said thickly, "are you very sure? I can still turn back."

"Don't. Please." Her words were slurred. "I've never been more sure of anything in my life."

"Ahh, Alice." He bent his head to nuzzle her neck, and his fingers touched her stomach lightly, drawing a sensuous line slowly downward. He moved to suckle her breasts as his fingers found her core of femininity.

She gasped as the fingers moved gently, insistently. "Relax, love, and flow with it," he murmured. Her face flushed hot, and perspiration beaded her brow as the final barrier came tumbling down. All her long denied senses came to life, and she felt moist, heavy, ripe for the taking. Her body arched upward to his touch, riding on the waves of passion that burst over her. Her breath came in short, hot gasps.

He felt the awakening of her body with a sense of awe. Already he had received the gifts of her spirit—her joy in simple pleasures, her sense of humor, her thirsting for knowledge. And now she was giving him the final treasure—her virginity. A tenderness unlike any he had ever known filled his heart, and he knew that this moment was forever seared into his memory.

Alice moaned beneath him. She was fully aroused, aching with the need for him. "Lance," she pleaded as the spasms of heat controlled her.

In a bright, golden haze of pleasure she felt his

fingers slip from her, felt the silken hair of his chest press against her breasts as his body covered hers, felt his heavy tumescence searching, probing. Ecstasy, laced with the first shocking pain of being known, ripped through her as his hot flesh entered her. Her fingers gripped his shoulders, holding on to solid reality as the rest of her body went spiraling off into a magic world of multicolored lights, blazing comets, and pleasure almost too sweet to bear. And when the lights went completely out of focus, when the fiery comet burned through her from head to toe, when the pleasant agony could no longer be borne, Lance carried her to the mountaintop and released her until she floated, limp and free, on a cloud of contentment.

His hand brushed her damp hair away from her forehead. "Alice. My sweet Alice," he murmured tenderly as his lips touched her love-slick flesh.

She focused her languid eyes on his face. "I love you, Lance," she whispered.

His eyes darkened. "Alice," he protested.

"Shhh." She put her fingertips against his lips. "Don't say anything. It doesn't matter." Tenderly, she moved her fingers across his face, memorizing its lines. "I know you don't love me . . . and I don't expect you to." Cupping his face in both hands she gazed seriously into his eyes. "I have to say it. I love you, Sir Lancelot, my golden knight. I'll always love you."

"I can't make a commitment. I thought you knew that before . . ."

"I did. I do." She pulled his head down to her breasts and stroked his hair. "Ahh, Lance. You've shown me such pleasure! You've opened a wonderful, magic door for me, and now that I've seen the other side I don't ever want to go back."

They lay quietly together on the jungle floor until the sun dropped off the western edge of the world. Lance stood and gathered their clothes. Extending a hand, he said to Alice, "Come."

She took his hand, shy at first of her nakedness, and then bold as she remembered what had passed between them. Together, they walked back to the camp. With the habits of civilization strong in her, Alice started to put on her clothes.

"Don't." Lance put a restraining hand on her arm. "Your body is lovely. I want to see you that way."

"We have to eat and . . . and . . ."

He chuckled. "There's nobody here to see us."

"But . . ."

"There's a lot that I can teach you, Alice. Let me."

She was quiet for a long moment, just looking at him. And then she smiled. "Do you mind if I put on my glasses? I don't want to miss a thing."

Lance threw back his head and roared with laughter. "Did anybody ever tell you that you have a bawdy sense of humor?"

"Is that bad?" she asked coyly.

"No. Delightful."

"If you hadn't said that, I was going to bash your head with a rock."

"The same rock you threatened me with before?"

"That's the one."

"I think we should frame that rock and hang it on a wall somewhere." He studied her for a long moment and then walked slowly, purposefully, toward her.

Her breath caught in her throat as he pulled her into his arms. "Like a trophy?" she whispered.

"Precisely." He covered her swollen lips with his and murmured, "The second time will be better for you."

And it was. Oh, how it was, she thought dreamily as she lay in the crook of his arm inside the tent. Her glasses winked at her from the tent floor, but that didn't matter. She hadn't needed them to see all the things he had taught her, things she had thought existed only in books with naughty covers. She giggled.

"What's so funny?" Lance caught a strand of her hair between his fingers and lazily brought it to his lips.

"I didn't know real people did that."

"That what?"

"I can't say it aloud."

"There will be no secrets in this camp, ma'am," he said with mock severity.

She leaned over and whispered in his ear. A huge grin split his face. "Oh, *that*," he said.

"Yes. Will you show me again?"

"Now?"

"Yes."

"Ma'am, you're an insatiable hoyden, a regular glutton. What do you think I am?" His eyes were twinkling as he teased her.

"My knight in tarnished armor."

"Oh well . . ." He rolled over and covered her body with his. "Since you put it that way, how can I refuse?"

A long while later he asked in a thick voice, "Is that what you meant?"

She smiled seductively at him. "No."

"No?"

"No. This is what I meant." And she showed him.

*　　*　　*

The jungle was dark as pitch and filled with the sounds of nocturnal animals when they emerged from the small tent. Together, they selected a can from their stock of food and started a fire in the grill. After they ate, Lance settled her against him and they sat in companionable silence, watching an enormous moon ride high over the jungle. The coals in the grill burned low and finally became blackened ashes.

Taking Alice by the hand, Lance rose and led her back into the tent. And she finally knew what it was like to spend an entire night in the arms of the vagabond fisherman.

The next two days were glorious for the new lovers. They explored their surroundings together, discovered that they were both avid stargazers and early risers. Lance challenged her to a footrace, which she won. As punishment for such insubordination he gave her a swimming lesson in the knee-deep stream. Like children of nature they frolicked, often naked, in their jungle paradise.

Alice filed away vignettes in her memory— tender, humorous scenes, frozen in time, that she would have forever.

"Damned insect bit me."
"Where, Lance?"
"There."
"*There?*"
"Stop laughing, Alice. It's not funny."

"*Now*, Lance?"
"Yes. It's good for your health."

"Yesterday you told me it would improve my appetite."

"I'm creative."

"You can say that again!"

"I'm . . ."

"Don't talk, Lance. Create."

"I was afraid of being like Heather."

"I know, love. . . . I wish I could thank her."

"Why?"

"Do you know what it's like . . . being with a virgin . . . knowing the trust you've placed in me?"

"No. What's it like?"

"I feel like a king."

"Just look at that moon, Lance."

"I'm going to take you there."

"We don't have a spaceship."

"We don't need one."

"Lance . . . I wonder if the astronauts know about this remarkable method of flying?"

"Be quiet and concentrate on the spaceship."

"Is that what you call it?"

"*Alice.*"

"Lance, you know the bug that bit you?"

"Yes."

"It bit me too."

"Where?"

"There."

"Cunning little devil, isn't he?"

*   *   *

As the time for the arrival of the others approached, Lance and Alice discussed the jungle filming and their impending trips to New England and Colorado.

"I believe we can finish here in three days," Alice said, "and then we'll leave to film the fall line." She brushed a wrinkle from her walking shorts.

Lance nuzzled her neck. "I like you better without clothes."

"You're not listening to a word I'm saying," she scolded him. She meant to sound very proper and businesslike. Instead, she sounded dreamy.

"I can just concentrate on one thing at a time. Right now, it's you." His hands moved to the front of her blouse.

"They'll be arriving at any time." Her head lolled back on a limp neck, and a familiar liquid heat rushed through her body.

"We have time," he murmured as he carried her into the tent.

Later he grinned down at her. "We'll move our tent away from the rest."

"No."

"No?" He lifted his brows. "Whatever you say, love. I don't mind being the center of attention."

Alice buttoned her blouse. "We won't be . . ." She hesitated, her face coloring. "We won't be doing this while the rest of the crew is in the jungle. My private life is my own affair."

"I'll be the soul of discretion. I'll wait until the moon is waning, and then I'll creep into your tent." He managed to keep his tone light, teasing. Dammit all, he thought, he would miss her.

"My mind is made up." She touched his cheek lightly. "I'll just have to suffer."

His heart wrenched at her choice of words.

That was the last thing he wanted. He didn't want to hurt Alice, not in any way. If denying herself for a few days caused suffering, what would she do when the filming was over and he went his lonely way? Funny. He had never thought of his life as being lonely.

She smiled at him from beneath the wing of soft hair that draped across her cheek. "When we get to New England and a proper hotel perhaps you'll want to pay me a visit."

"Perhaps," he said nonchalantly.

"I've heard more enthusiasm from people waiting in dentist's offices." She twisted her hair into a knot and put on her glasses.

He held his hands up in mock surrender. "I confess, ma'am. Wild horses couldn't keep me away."

"It's a good thing you said that. I still have my rock."

An hour later the crew arrived in two rented vans, and everybody got down to the serious business of filming Eduardo's line of casual wear. Lance looked unusually magnificent in the jungle setting, and Alice had a hard time keeping her mind on the commercials. He compounded the problem by sneaking up at the most unexpected moments, nuzzling her neck and whispering improper remarks when no one was looking. The nights were even worse. She missed Lance. She missed their midnight conversations. Even the most inconsequential topics had been exciting when infused with his quick wit. But most of all she missed being in his arms.

The crew worked hard to finish the jungle filming. Linda said she could hardly wait to get to New England for the fall filming. She was tired of jungle heat and jungle insects. Mattie suggested they skip New England and go straight to Colorado for the winter line. She wanted to try her hand at skiing.

Their last night in the Yucatán jungle was a celebration, with Lance manning the grill and Mattie preparing a concoction that she called a mystery salad. Alex had stowed several bottles of tequila on the van, and after a couple of drinks Linda and one of the camera crew did an impromptu dance everybody dubbed the Mexican hatless dance.

In the wee hours of the morning, when the tequila bottles were empty and the diners were melancholy, everybody agreed that the mystery of Mattie's salad was why no one had died from eating it. Mattie cheerfully passed around a box of antacid tablets, billing them as after-dinner mints.

After everyone had said good night Alice lay inside her tent, wide awake. She knew that she would never forget the jungle, for it was here that she had given herself completely and irrevocably to Lancelot. Who was he, this mystery man who had stolen her heart? Just before sleep claimed her, she recalled a brief conversation they had had one afternoon beside the stream. "Who are you?" she had asked. "I'm Lancelot," he had replied. "What do you believe in?" "I believe in whoever I am at the moment." With the sudden flash of insight that often comes in that moment between complete consciousness and sleep, she realized that she, too, believed in whoever Lancelot was at the moment. Smiling, she closed her eyes and slept.

When the morning sun peeked down on the campsite nothing was stirring except a brilliantly plummaged parrot that had come to investigate a leftover lettuce leaf.

Eight

Alice stood on a Colorado mountaintop and watched the crew loading the equipment onto the vans. She couldn't believe that tomorrow would be their last day of filming. Their short stay in the Green Mountains of Vermont was now only a golden haze in her memory, and the glorious interlude in Vail was almost over.

She lifted her face to the snow-capped mountain peaks, and her breath made small clouds in the frigid air. She wasn't ready for it to end. A small tear slid from the corner of her eye as the line of vans started down the mountainside.

She suddenly felt Lance's hands on her shoulders. "Ready, love?" he asked. "Our chariot awaits."

"Yes." She dashed the tear away, hoping he wouldn't see.

He didn't miss a thing. His gaze roamed over her face as he turned her in his arms. Tilting her chin up with one finger, he asked softly, "What's wrong?"

"I'm scared," she confessed, "scared of how I'll handle the loneliness."

For a moment his face was open, vulnerable, and Alice caught a fleeting glimpse of something that looked very much like her own fear. And then, so quickly that it might never have been there, the emotion was gone, replaced by a smooth mask.

"Alice, Alice." He crushed her against his chest and rested his chin on her soft hair. "You're a strong, beautiful woman. You can handle anything."

"I'm not." She rubbed her face against his chest, feeling the wool scratch against her cheek. "I'm not beautiful." And then, because she didn't want her weakness to make him feel guilty and trapped, she pretended a bravado that she didn't feel. "But I *am* strong. I can handle anything." She lifted her head and tenderly touched his cheek. "Anything, Lance."

He felt a pang at the sight of her brave, lovely face, and he was certain she was unaware that a second tear had stolen from the corner of her eye. He took her hands and lifted them to his lips, kissing her gloved fingertips.

"You *are* beautiful, Alice, beautiful in a way that few women are. You have a beauty of soul and mind. A lovely innocence. And remarkable courage. You're beautiful inside, and that's the kind of beauty that counts."

"The face that launched a thousand ships, huh?" she said jokingly.

"Yes, Alice. The face that launched a thousand ships." He dropped her hands and gently traced her cheekbones with his fingers. "You have the kind of beauty that poets extol, the kind of loveliness that men write home about. You're warm and

sweet and cuddly. You're fun and sexy and sometimes as tart as a good, crisp apple. Any man would
be proud to have you by his side."

Except you, she thought forlornly. "I guess I'll
just have to find a man who likes apples as a
steady diet," she said, forcing a lightness into
her voice.

"You will." He looked at her brave smile and felt a
sudden pang of jealousy of that man. Damn, he
thought. What was wrong with him? Did he think
he could have his cake and eat it too? He had made
his choices a long time ago.

Taking her elbow, he led her to the minivan. "In
the meantime," he said, "would you settle for a
half-frozen male model with an enormous hankering for a cup of hot chocolate?"

She laughed. One of the things she loved most
about him was his ability to make her laugh.
"Hankering?"

He revved the engine and roared off down the
mountain. "It's—"

"I know," she interrupted.

". . . an old Southern saying," they said
simultaneously.

Their merriment dispelled the somber mood,
and they were still laughing when they entered the
hotel. Lance took her hand and propelled her
toward the elevator. "Follow me, love. I have something to show you."

She rubbed her cheek against the front of his
scratchy wool jacket. "What is it?"

"You'll see." He whisked her down the hall and
into his room, and gathered her into his arms.

"What about the hot chocolate?"

"Later."

They never did get around to the hot chocolate.

* * *

A small sound awakened Alice, and she sat up in Lance's bed. The room was dark except for the faint glow from the sunset coming through their window. She opened her mouth to call to Lance, then stopped. He was standing beside the window, his profile etched against the dying sun. He seemed to be looking at something far in the distance, and even across the room she could sense the cloak of sadness that wrapped around him. Her heart stood still as she watched him. She wanted to rush into his arms, to comfort him, but instinctively she knew that his thoughts were private, that he would not welcome the intrusion.

With a wild rush of happiness, she wondered if he was deciding not to leave her when the filming was over. Her nerve endings stretched as tight as violin strings as she sat on the bed, waiting. She could almost hear time marching by in storm-trooper boots.

Slowly, Lance turned from the window. Seeing her, he smiled. She uttered a smothered cry and bounded across the room. Putting her arms around his naked waist, she squeezed as hard as she could. "I'm here, Lance," she said softly.

"I know." He pulled her closer and rubbed his chin against her hair. The minutes crept slowly by in the deafening silence.

At last he loosened his grip and smiled down at her. "I'm starved. How about you?"

"Ravenous," she agreed, turning quickly so he wouldn't see the disappointment on her face. The moment that might have been had passed. The moment when Lance stood on the brink of confession and commitment was lost forever, and the two of them were shuttled safely back to their private, lonely worlds.

The view from the restaurant was breathtaking, and Alice stared as if she were seeing the snow-covered mountains for the first time. Although Lance was attempting to keep a light banter going, her heart wasn't in it. She kept seeing him standing at the bedroom window, staring into space as if it held the solutions to his dilemma. Was he beginning to feel something for her? she wondered. Was she more than another woman to warm his bed? With each passing day, her love for him had grown. It didn't matter that his background was still a mystery. She had seen the man that he was, the warm, wonderful, patient man, with a quick sense of humor and a wide streak of impulsiveness.

He reached across the table and clasped her hands. "You're a million miles away," he said.

She turned to look at him. The flickering candlelight cast an otherworldly glow on his bronze face, enhancing the image of remoteness and mystery.

"In a way, I am," she said. "I'm trying to be where you are—a million miles away from family and home and business ties and commitment." She saw a fleeting look of stunned disbelief on his face as she brazenly attacked his citadel of silence. Then his nonchalant mask dropped carefully into place.

"That's not a place you should be." He lifted his wineglass to his lips and took a casual sip.

"I don't seem to have any choice. I'm in love with you."

He said nothing, his eyes smoldering at her over the rim of his glass.

"Once," she continued, "you asked me to dare." She caught her lower lip between her teeth before going on. Was she pushing him too hard? Shouldn't she take her magic interlude and be content? But she knew she would never forgive herself if she didn't take this final dare. She had already risked her heart and lost it. No, not lost. Given it freely to her vagabond fisherman. Now she was risking her future on one throw of the dice, winner take all. She was gambling that her challenge would shake him into reassessing his life. She was risking the little time they had left together against a future, *their* future. "I'm asking you the same thing, Lance. Dare."

He laughed without mirth. "You're talking to the world's all-time champion daredevil. I've climbed mountains, braved jungles, and conquered the wilderness. I've gambled in Monte Carlo, raced the Grand Prix in France, and fought the bulls in Spain."

"But have you let yourself feel?"

"Hell, yes. I've felt elation and excitement and sometimes dog-tired weariness. I've been drunk and happy and sad. But most of all . . . I've been free."

She had her answer. She had gambled and lost. Lifting her wineglass, she proposed a toast. "To freedom." The words had a forlorn, hollow ring.

"To freedom." He drained his glass, then poured himself another. "And to Alice. A helluva classy lady."

She sipped her wine and rationalized. She hadn't lost, not really. It was impossible to lose what you never had. And she had never had Lance. All along she had been a temporary woman, just a warm body to fill the empty spot in his bed until he moved on to the next town or the next seaport or the next country. Damn! Love was sometimes a hurtful thing.

Alice never knew how she got through the rest of the meal. It must have been some age-old survival instinct that saved her from falling apart at the table. Lance escorted her in silence to her door. She didn't ask him to come in. Even if she had, she knew he would have declined. They both needed to be alone.

"Good night, Lance." She kissed him lightly on the lips.

"Sweet dreams, love." He held her chin for a long moment, gazing deep into her eyes. And then he was gone. He walked swiftly down the hall, hands crammed into his pockets and torso bent forward as if to hasten his exit.

Alice watched until he was swallowed up by the elevator. Inside her room, she busied herself with ordinary, mundane things, willing herself not to cry. She looked over her notes for tomorrow's shooting, shampooed her hair, and made an unprecedented call to Tom at his home to talk business. After the call was finished and her ears had stopped smarting she glanced down at her watch. It was only nine o'clock in Vail, but she had forgotten the time difference. Tom was probably still cursing.

She pulled on her white cotton gown and crawled into bed, flipping on the television with the remote control. An old murder mystery movie was on, and she tried to lose herself in the plot. After thirty minutes she gave up. She didn't give a damn who had done it. She didn't like the butler, and she didn't like the gardener, and the hero made her think of Lance.

Impatiently, she jumped out of bed and took a novel from her briefcase. She found her place in the middle of the book and read three chapters before she realized that she couldn't remember a word she had read. She started over. The minutes crept by on leaden feet, and from time to time she shook her watch to see if it was still running.

Finally she gave up and went to bed. She lay in the dark, staring at the ceiling. Lights from the glass-enclosed recreation area outside her balcony filtered into the room, making surrealistic shadows on her walls. She watched the shadows for a long time, then wearily closed her eyes. She dreamed of racing across the plains on a white stallion, chasing a knight in shining, golden armor. But no matter how hard she raced the golden knight stayed just out of her reach.

Lance watched the crew pack up their gear for the last time. The filming was over, and for the last few days he had been waiting for the familiar restless stirrings within himself, the yearning for new places and new people. Maybe he was getting old, he thought as he climbed into the minivan beside Mattie and Linda. Too old to hear the siren song of wanderlust.

"Ready, ladies?" he asked, glancing at his companions. If he and Alice hadn't discussed commitment and freedom last night, she would be sitting beside him now. Instead, she was in the other van with Alex. He revved the engine and shook his head. Life was full of might-have-beens.

Mattie massaged her bruised arms. "If I don't see another mountain for the next fifty years, it'll be too soon for me." She scowled at Lance, not because she was angry, but because scowling was her way of camouflaging a tender heart. "What makes an old fool like me stand on a pair of sticks three inches wide and try to slide down a mountain?"

"Adventure, Mattie." Lance smiled at her. He was going to miss her sharp tongue and bawdy sense of humor. He was going to miss all of them. He felt a queer tugging at his heart as he shut his mind against the one he would miss most of all. That was over and done with now. Past history. It was too late for regrets. He hadn't meant to hurt Alice, and he would carry the guilt with him for the rest of his life. Guilt, and something else. He wouldn't put a name to that something else, he decided. If he did, his freedom would be gone forever.

He parked the van beside the hotel and the three of them got out. "So long, ladies," he said. "It's been fun working with you."

"Won't we be seeing you again, Lancelot?" Linda asked, her eyes round with wonder.

"No. I'm moving on."

"Gosh, I thought—" Linda clapped her hand over her mouth to keep from saying what she thought. It was none of her business, she decided as she waved her hand and went inside the hotel.

Mattie put her hands on her hips. She wasn't fooled for one minute. "The grass is always greener, eh?"

Lance leaned against the side of the van. "Something like that."

"I knew a man like you once." She cocked her head to one side and studied him for a moment. "He left a wife, a home, and friends who loved him to chase rainbows in faraway places. He ended up sick and penniless in a fleabag hotel a thousand miles from home. He died a lonely, disillusioned man." She stopped talking to see if her words made any impact on him. Apparently they hadn't, for his face was still an unreadable mask. "That man was my husband."

"I'm sorry, Mattie."

"I am, too, Lance. Take care." Shaking her head, she left him standing beside the van.

When Alice stepped from her van Lance was still where Mattie had left him. She felt slightly dizzy as she looked at him, and she knew it wasn't the altitude. He would be leaving soon without saying good-bye. He wasn't the kind of man who indulged in tearful farewells. She couldn't let him go like this. She didn't want him to remember her the way she had been last night, prompting him on the subject of commitment. She wanted him to remember her without guilt. She wanted him to think of her as an independent woman who made her own choices and wasn't afraid of the consequences. She wanted him to remember her as a woman smiling and laughing, a woman who lost gracefully.

Smiling bravely, she approached him. "I've come to wish you good luck on your next venture, Lance."

He smiled that slow, lazy smile that always melted her right down to her toes. "Thank you." They stood in silence with the bright November sun washing over them. When the tension between them became a palpable thing he reached out and touched her cheek. "I'm sorry, Alice," he said softly. "I never meant to hurt you."

"Please, Lance." She took his hand and brushed it lightly with her lips, then released it and smiled at him. "You didn't hurt me. You gave me the greatest joy a woman can know. I have no regrets. I couldn't let you go without telling you that."

"You're a woman of courage, Miss Alice Spencer."

No, she thought. She was just a woman who knew how to pick up the pieces and go on living. She had done it after Heather's death, and she could do it again. But if she didn't leave quickly, she would fall apart. She couldn't stand this close to him another minute without collapsing in his arms and begging him to come back to Boston with her.

"Thank you, Lance. Good-bye." She turned and hurried to the hotel.

"Adios," she heard him call after her. Even his good-bye had to wear a mask, she thought.

Alice sat on the cutting-room floor, surrounded by discarded film. Her back ached, her head hurt, and she wanted to scream in helpless frustration. She had been back in Boston for two weeks, and today had been the first time she had seen the footage of Lance. Until now she hadn't been able to bear the thought of editing the film. Tom would have done it, but these commercials were her baby. Dammit all, she thought, if she couldn't make herself look at his picture without swooning, how could she expect to put him behind her and get on with the business of ordinary living?

She rose and threaded a section of the film back onto the projector. Lance in the jungle, surrounded by tropical foliage, smiling into the camera. Alice's knees went weak with remembrance, and she had to sit down. As if it were only yesterday, she could feel again his smooth, golden flesh against hers, could hear the gentle murmur of water as they made love beside the stream. Putting her hands to her flushed face, she moaned. Why had she let herself fall in love with a vagabond?

She rewound the film and tried to concentrate on her editing. The commercials were to be aired soon. She didn't have forever to indulge in fantasies. She came to the footage they had done at night. Lance's hair was tinted silver, just the way it had been when they had talked of flying to the moon. She clutched the back of a chair as a white-hot longing shot through her. Oh, Lord, she wanted to be in his arms. She wanted to fly to the moon with him once more.

She walked shakily to the water fountain and took a sip. The cool liquid did nothing to quench the fires that were burning within her. Taking a deep breath, she forced herself back to her task. As she alternately edited and swooned, she decided that she deserved the Congressional Medal of Honor for bravery above and beyond the call of duty.

She was emotionally and physically drained when she got home that night. Her house was filled with the wonderful smell of freshly baked bread, and she could hear Mrs. B humming in the kitchen. She stuck her head through the door. "Any mail today?" she asked hopefully.

"A bill from the insurance company. I put it on the hall table." Mrs. B turned from the chicken she was preparing for baking. "You look terrible." She wiped her hands on a damp towel and walked over to Alice. "You're white as a sheet. Come over here and sit down." She led Alice to a chair and bustled about the kitchen, making her a cup of hot tea.

"Now drink this and tell me why you've been moping about since you got home from Colorado."

"I've just been working too hard," Alice said evasively. She didn't know whether she was ready to talk about Lance. Not even to Mrs. B.

"You thrive on hard work," Mrs. B said. She pursed her lips. "What's the real reason you've looked like death on wheels these last two weeks?"

"You sound like Mattie." Alice attempted a weak smile over the rim of her teacup. "Where's Mark?"

"Mark is over at Jimmy's. Sylvia's bringing him home at seven. Now tell me what's wrong." She poured herself a cup of tea and sat down beside Alice.

"What about the chicken?"

"The chicken can wait." The clock on the kitchen wall ticked loudly in the silence, until Alice finally gave in.

"It's Lance." Her voice broke on his name, and a small tear trembled on the end of her eyelash. She removed her glasses and brushed it away.

"I thought so." Mrs. B placed her hand over Alice's. "You love him, don't you?"

"Yes. How did you know?"

"I knew before I left Mexico. It didn't take a genius to figure it out."

"Was I that obvious?"

"Only to me. But then, you're like my own child."

"He made me feel . . ." She groped for the right words to describe how she had felt with Lance. There were none, she decided. How can you describe flying-to-the-moon magic? ". . . things I've never felt before. For the first time in my life I felt alive. Giddy. Happy." She covered her face with her hands, remembering. "How could I have been so foolish?"

"Feeling alive and happy isn't foolish."

"Falling in love with the wrong man is."

"How do you know he's the wrong man?"

Alice lifted her head. "He's a drifter. He has no name, no home, no background. What kind of future is there with a man like that?"

"With a man like that . . ." Mrs. B paused. "With a man like that it sometimes takes longer to know the heart. Give him time, Alice. If the love is meant to be, he'll come back to you."

"I don't think so. Just look at me. Why would a gorgeous man like Lance want a woman like me when he could have anybody in the world?"

"Now I won't hear such talk," Mrs. B scolded. "You're a beautiful woman."

"I'm nearsighted and flat-chested and my hair is mousy brown. Heather was the beauty."

"Poppycock!" Mrs. B exploded. She rarely raised her voice and never said a bad word. Poppycock was her cussword, and when she said it Alice knew she was really angry. "I think it's about time for you to stop hiding. Lance found that soft, lovely woman. Let her come on out. Get rid of those glasses. Let your hair down. And get a swimsuit besides that old menopause blue one you wore in Mexico!" Mrs. B's face was red from her unaccustomed anger.

Alice listened in astonishment. Her smile was tentative at first, then it turned into a broad grin. She chuckled. "Where will I find a new swimsuit? It's the dead of winter."

"We'll go to Florida over the Christmas holidays and buy you one." Mrs. B rose from her chair, smiling, and put the chicken in the oven. "That's just two weeks away. You won't be swimming between now and then." She set the timer and turned back to Alice. "Lance is a good man, Alice. I know. I watched him with Mark. Any man who loves kids that way can't be bad."

"No, he wasn't bad," Alice said softly. "He was wonderful. And he never made promises he didn't keep."

"You're more levelheaded than your sister was. You didn't make a bad choice, and it's time for you to put all that behind you."

Alice knew that Mrs. B was right. She had laid the ghost of Heather to rest in the jungle before she gave herself to Lancelot. Why resurrect it now? It was time to get on with her life. It was time to finish what Lance had started, time to release the warm, sensual woman whom he had discovered, to free herself from the bonds of sensible clothes and severe hairstyle. She loved Lance. She always would. And if he came back, life would be wonderful. But even if he didn't come back, she wouldn't stop living. She would go on, a little wiser and a lot more experienced. And who knows, she thought. In time she might find somebody else. Somebody ready for commitment.

She crossed the kitchen and hugged Mrs. B. "Thank you."

"I believe he'll come back, Alice."

"I'm not going to hold my breath." She walked smartly toward the kitchen door, renewed vigor in her steps.

"That's my girl. Chin up and keep on fighting."

Alice twirled before the mirror in Annette's Boutique. With her new fluffy hairstyle and her contact lenses, she hardly recognized herself. The full skirt of the red wool dress swirled around her legs and called attention to the flirty red high heels she was wearing. "Hello, Alice Spencer," she said to her reflection. "Do I know you?" She giggled. What would everybody in the office say? Linda would probably faint. She turned to the salesgirl. "I'll take it."

"Very good, madam." The slender, dark-haired girl held up a strapless black satin dress with a sequined jacket. "And this one?"

What the heck, Alice thought. She might as well go all the way. "I'll take it too." She arranged for the black dress to be delivered after alterations and wore the red dress home.

When she walked through her front door she automatically reached for her sensible felt hat. Then she remembered that she didn't wear sensible felt hats anymore. Grinning broadly, she turned to the hall table and riffled through the day's mail. Suddenly she froze. There was no mistaking the bold handwriting. She turned the card over and read, "Thinking of you, Lance." She ran her fingers over his signature and was overwhelmed with such longing that she had to grasp the edge of the table.

Clutching the card to her chest, she ran upstairs to her bedroom. Tears blurred her eyes as she looked at the card. "Dammit, Lance," she whispered, "why did you even bother to write? I was just getting used to the idea of living without you." Liar, her mind screamed. You'll never get used to the idea of being without Lance. He's spoiled you for any other man.

She wiped her face with the back of her hand. What was the use of moping? He was probably at the other end of the world by now, chasing elusive dreams. The card was postmarked California, but that didn't mean a thing. He never stayed in one place long enough to have an address.

Alice was subdued during dinner, and even Mrs. B didn't try to find out what was wrong. After dinner Alice helped Mark with his homework, then tried to concentrate on the work she had brought home from the office. She finally gave up, said good night to Mrs. B, and went up to her bedroom.

Lance's card was where she had left it on the bed. She put on a blue silk nightgown, then stood in front of the mirror, brushing her hair and attempting to forget about the card and its sender. It was useless. She threw the brush across the room. "Get out of my life, Lancelot," she muttered.

Marching to the bed, she picked up his card, tore it in half, and let the two pieces flutter into the wastebasket. "Good-bye, Lancelot." She turned out the light and crawled into bed, but it was a long time before she slept.

The next day she puttered around the house, listening to the Saturday-morning cartoons and trying not to think about the torn card in her wastebasket. Everytime she went into her bedroom she carefully avoided looking in that direction. Dammit, she fumed, he had no right to mess up her life.

She paid her monthly bills, addressed her Christmas cards, and cleaned the kitchen cabinets. She dropped Mark and his friend off at a matinee and had a late lunch of Campbell's chicken soup over Mrs. B's strong objections. Ignoring the dire prediction that she would get skinny as a snake eating like that, Alice then marched up to the attic to search for a treetop angel that she had stored there years ago.

Mrs. B called up the stairs after her, "What's put such a bee in your bonnet?"

"I'm just looking for the angel. That's all," Alice yelled down.

"If you ask me, you're running from something. Isn't it time for you to pick up Mark?"

"Sylvia's bringing them home."

Mrs. B labored up the attic stairs and poked her head through the opening. "I thought I should tell you. I found Lance's card in your wastebasket."

Alice lifted her head from inside a dusty trunk. "That's where I want it to be."

"He's coming back. I know he is."

"He's out of my life." She bent over and scrambled through the trunk once more. "Even if he came back, I wouldn't see him. He's totally unreliable."

"What did you say? I can't hear you with your head in that trunk."

"I said," she yelled, jerking her head out of the trunk, "that I don't give a damn whether he ever comes back. He can just chase moonbeams for the rest of his life. I don't care."

"I see." Mrs. B pursed her lips and went quietly down the stairs.

After dinner that night Alice was still whirling around the house as if chased by demons. Mark and Mrs. B were watching a television Christmas special in the den.

"Look," Mark suddenly shouted. "There's Lance."

Alice stuck her head around the kitchen door, and there he was, smiling from the television screen. The snow-capped Colorado mountains rose behind him and the sun tinted his hair gold. She swallowed a lump in her throat and bolted up the stairs to her room. Damn him, she thought. Damn him for still being able to make her body burn with desire. Why couldn't she forget him? After all these weeks why couldn't he be just a pleasant memory? She leaned against her bedroom door until her knees stopped shaking, and then walked to her wastebasket and picked up his torn Christmas card. Carefully she placed it on the table and fitted the pieces together. With tears blinding her eyes, she searched her bedside table for the tape. Her hands closed over the plastic dispenser, and she tore off a strip. The *a* and the *n* fit together crookedly, but at least the card was in one piece. She held it to her chest and let the tears spill down her face unchecked.

Her bedroom door eased open and Mark walked into her room. "I've come to say good night, Aunt Alice." He stopped when he saw her face. "Why are you crying?"

She looked at the small boy and held out her arms. "Come here, darling. It has nothing to do with you." She hugged him close. "Do you remember the times you felt sad and I told you that it was all right for boys to cry?"

His eyes went solemn as he nodded his head.

"Well, sometimes grown-ups feel sad too."

"Is it all right for grown-ups to cry?"

"Yes, Mark. It's all right for grown-ups to cry."

Nine

A week later Alice remembered her words to Mark as she stood gazing out her office window. Yes, she thought, it was all right for grown-ups to cry. It meant that they still were capable of feeling. At least some of them were. As she watched shoppers laden with Christmas packages scurrying home to their families, she wondered about Lance. What was he doing now? Did he have family he went home to at Christmas, or did he even allow himself that much feeling?

"I'm going home now, Alice."

She turned at the sound of Tom's voice. "Have a happy holiday, Tom."

"You too. I'll see you after the first."

She walked back to her desk and sat down. She needed to review the storyboards for the dog-food commercials they would be shooting after Christmas. Forgetting the time as she often did when she was working, she stayed until all her office personnel had gone home. She kicked off her red high heels and tucked her feet up under her red wool skirt. She was so intent on the storyboards that she didn't hear the knock at her door.

"I knew you would still be here," a man's voice said. "You look lovely, Alice."

A tidal wave of emotion washed over her at the sound of that familiar drawl. Slowly, she lifted her head, and there he was, her vagabond fisherman, leaning against her doorway as if he were in the habit of casually dropping by. His usually tousled blond hair was combed neatly into place and his beat-up jeans had been replaced by a three-piece business suit. She gripped the edge of her desk for support. Squelching an urge to rush into his arms, she made herself remember his long silence, his unpredictable nature.

"Hello, Lance." She congratulated herself on her calmness. Her gaze took in his cream-colored shirt, his silk tie. "Or should I say, 'Hello, somebody else.' You don't look like Lance." Her knuckles were turning white from her tight grip on the desk. Her love was standing in her office, and yet he was not her vagabond fisherman. Except for the same rakish smile, this man was someone else, someone she didn't know. "Who are you this time?"

"Craig." With the loose-jointed grace that she remembered so well, he crossed to a chair and sat down.

"Not King Arthur?"

"I've given up fictitious names."

Her heart pounded so hard that she was sure he could hear it across the room. He had given up fictitious names, she thought. Did she dare hope . . . She smothered the thought before it became full-blown. Her wounds weren't healed from their last encounter. Why open herself to more heartbreak?

"For how long?" she asked.

"Forever." He sat in the chair, watching her quietly, until the tension in the room became unbearable. Then he rose quickly and came to her. Lifting her by the shoulders, he pulled her into his arms. "Forever," he whispered into her soft hair.

Alice leaned her head against his chest and inhaled the fresh, wind-whipped fragrance of him. She wanted to believe him. She wanted to wrap her arms around his neck and never let go. "Why should I believe you?" she asked.

His arms tightened around her. "I thought I could get you out of my mind. After you left Colorado I went to California, to Squaw Valley. I tried to tell myself how wonderful it felt to ski down the mountainside. No ties, no commitments. Free as a bird. It didn't work, my darling."

Her heart thundered in her ears. Caution was strong in her as she lifted her head so that she could see his face. He had called her darling before. It didn't mean a thing. Her mouth went dry at the sight of his stunningly handsome face looming so close. "I don't even know you."

"I know," he said quietly. "I'm not here to renew an affair, Alice. I'm here so that you can get to know me, the real me." Tenderly, he cupped her upturned face with his right hand. "I'm here to court the woman I love."

Alice should have been ecstatic. She wasn't. Those were the words she had longed to hear. If Lance had told her a month ago that he loved her, she would have taken wing and flown to the moon. But a man named Craig was saying them now, a man she didn't even know. "I fell in love with Lancelot."

His thumb gently circled her cheek. "Give me a

chance, Alice. I'll make you love Craig Beaufort too."

She sucked in her breath. "Of the Beaufort publishing empire?"

"The same," he said quietly.

That explained a lot of things about Lancelot, she thought. Beaufort Publishing was a large, highly successful company. It published several magazines and newspapers, and also had a list of best-selling hardcover books. "But I'm not the same woman either," she said. "Thanks to you, I'm more experienced, wiser, I hope."

"You will always be my courageous love." She almost drowned in the blue of his eyes as his head bent closer. "And I will always be your knight in tarnished armor." His lips captured hers, achingly sweet and unbearably tender.

She curled her hands into his hair as the familiar languour stole over her. She had thought she would never feel his lips again, never know again the magic of being held in his arms. If Craig Beaufort had said the word, in that heady moment she would have followed him to the ends of the earth. "Lance, Lance, my love," she murmured as she pressed her body closer to his.

He abruptly lifted his head. "Dammit, I'm not Lancelot. I'm Craig Beaufort."

Alice went on the defensive immediately. "Well, you certainly kiss like Lancelot!" She whirled around and marched to her chair. "Just what do you think gives you the right to come here after all these weeks of silence and disrupt my life? I'm not that eager virgin you knew in Mexico."

Craig's eyes gleamed in appreciation of her spunk. No wonder he hadn't forgotten Alice, he thought. There wasn't another woman in the world who could land on her feet so quickly. He was reminded of the day he had first met her. She hadn't batted an eyelash about boarding that old lobster boat in her proper suit and high heels.

He sat back down, stretched his long legs out before him, and smiled. "You have every right to be mad as hell, Alice. I wouldn't blame you if you threw me out on my tail." He winked at her. "But I hope you won't."

The wink almost undid her. Except for the suit, at that moment he looked pure vagabond fisherman. She picked up a pencil and doodled on the edge of a file folder, giving herself time to regain her composure. Dammit, she thought, she never doodled. What was that man doing to her? "Give me one good reason why I shouldn't."

"If you do, you'll never know why I was on that lobster boat."

"Why *were* you on that boat?" She put the pencil in its holder and propped her elbows on the desk. She refused to become a doodler just because Lancelot-Craig was sitting across the room from her, making her mouth go dry.

"It seemed a good place to be at the time."

"You'll have to do better than that. That's no explanation."

"If you want to hear the rest of the story, you'll have to come to dinner with me."

"Just like that?" She snapped her fingers. "You come drifting in here from heaven knows where and I'm supposed to come when you whistle?"

"Did I whistle?"

"Don't play word games with me," she snapped.

"As I recall," he drawled, grinning, "you used to like games. Footraces in the nude and rocket ships to the moon."

His words brought back memories so vivid that a molten, liquid heat poured through her body and settled in the juncture of her thighs. "Your tongue always was as golden as your hair. I'm not impressed anymore, Craig." She pressed her legs together, willing the heat to subside, and wondered if liars were ever struck dead by lightning. She hoped not.

"Still Alice of the tart tongue?"

"That's me. Alice the Apple." Why did everything he say remind her of those magic moments they had shared on location? Was he doing it deliberately?

"I've made reservations for us at Maître Jacques," he said.

"Mrs. B is expecting me. I must decline." She needed time to think about all this. It would be foolish to rush headlong into heartbreak again.

He rose from his chair with unhurried grace and pulled her coat from the closet. Then he walked behind her desk, towering over her, smiling. "I've taken care of everything. Mrs. B has given us her blessing."

"How dare you preempt my plans?" Secretly, she was pleased. More and more, Craig Beaufort was revealing the Lancelot characteristics she had loved so well.

"Your coat, love. We're already fashionably late." She put her shoes back on and stood, and as she slipped her arms into the coat, he leaned down and whispered into her ear, "I dare many things, darling. Or have you forgotten?"

Had she forgotten? Heavens no! Not even brainwashing could make her forget. But if Craig Beaufort thought she was going to come tumbling back into his bed at the crook of a finger, he had better think again. This time around Alice Spencer was going to play hard to get!

She felt light-headed as they stepped into a cab. How many times had she dreamed about Lancelot returning? How many times had she pictured that golden-wheat hair and those electric blue eyes? There was something different about him, though, besides the clothes. He was less relaxed, and there was a feeling of power about him, almost as if his body housed a pulsing dynamo.

She leaned her head back on the seat and waited for him to make his move, to reach out and touch her cheek, or, better yet, her thigh. She quivered with anticipation, then smiled as she imagined his shock when she pushed him away. Let him suffer a little the way she had these last few weeks! If that sounded vindictive, it was also human, she decided. She was no plaster saint.

Craig casually draped his arm across the back of the seat and pretended to look out the window. That kiss back there in the office had been a mistake, he decided. As much as he wanted to grab Alice and run to the nearest bed, he knew it would be a rerun of her affair with Lancelot. Dammit, he had to make her love the real man, Craig Beaufort, businessman. He didn't want just her body. He wanted all of her. He wanted her indomitable spirit, her tart tongue, her questing mind. He wanted that deep reservoir of warmth. He wanted her to love him with every ounce of her being.

Alice looked at the distance that separated them and frowned. She had meant to play hard to get, but not that hard. It was beginning to look as if she would need Mrs. B's blessing after all. What would the cabdriver think if she unbuttoned Lance's shirt and ran her fingers over his golden chest?

she wondered. That was what she wanted to do. And what did that make her? Some kind of hussy? She scowled and looked out the window. Well hell, she wasn't made of steel either. Just look at her, she fumed, one hour in his company and she was already hot as a cat on a tin roof and cussing like a stevedore. She stole a glance at the composed golden man sitting beside her. Dammit, he wasn't even Lance.

Her smile was somewhat thin when Craig escorted her into the restaurant. The maître d' had his nose so high in the air, Alice was surprised he didn't ask for their pedigree. She was even miffed at the rose on the table. What was all the fuss about red roses?

The maître d' indicated the rose. "For the lady. A small remembrance of an unforgettable dining experience." He gave her a toothy smile.

"I prefer orchids," she snapped.

"But we thank you anyhow," Craig said smoothly.

The maître d' stretched his neck two inches higher and peered disapprovingly down his beak nose before leaving.

"So you prefer orchids?" Craig asked, smiling at her.

She didn't know whether to be grateful or mad. Lancelot would have teased her about her lack of Southern manners. She conceded that she had needed rescuing from her incredible lapse in self-control. "Yes, I prefer orchids," she said. "They remind me of exotic, faraway places."

Alice had always appeared perfectly at ease in her roles of surrogate mother and stable business-woman, Craig thought. It surprised him to catch a glimpse of wanderlust in her eyes. Perhaps she had more in common with Lancelot than he had realized. He would have to explore that possibility. "Have you ever longed to go to any of those places?" he asked.

Forgetting her surroundings, thinking only of how easy it had been in the jungle to confide in this man with his compelling eyes, she leaned across the table. "Everyone has dreams. Don't you think so? When I was growing up I used to go to Evans Pond to ice skate. I dreamed of being a professional ice skater and traveling the world." She didn't realize how her face sparkled when she spoke of her dream. She propped her chin on her cupped palms. "Tell me your dreams, Craig Beaufort."

"I dreamed of having a father who would play ball in the backyard and take me on picnics to the park." He spoke lightly, but Alice could see the shadows in his eyes. Craig was opening the doors to his past in a way that Lancelot never had. "Instead, I had a dad who gave me life and a name. He loved his business first and his family on holidays."

"And your mother?"

"She learned early that the way to please Dad was to achieve prominence in the community. I rarely saw her except in the society pages of the newspaper." He picked up his menu. "What would you like for dinner? The Dover sole is very good here."

"Dover sole gives me hives," she said absently. It seemed strangely out of character that Craig was familiar with this very formal restaurant. Her Lancelot had always seemed more at home in jeans at a seaside picnic. There was obviously much she had to learn about this businessman in the three-piece suit. "You still haven't told me why you were on that lobster boat."

"And you still haven't told me what you want for dinner."

"Craig! You promised."

"I also promised to court you properly, love. How would you like to hear a love song?" There was an almost audible click as he closed the door to further conversation about his past.

Alice decided that she could be patient. Rome wasn't built in a day, and neither could a relationship spring full-blown between herself and this man who was part familiar lover, part stranger. She'd play it his way. Only, Lord, she wished he'd hurry with the preliminaries. Even if she was playing hard to get, she didn't want to be forty when he got her. "You sing?" she asked.

"Only in the shower."

Her face flushed. Here it comes, she thought. The invitation to his shower. She'd make it easier for him. "I'm disappointed," she said. "I wanted to hear you." She could hardly believe she had said those bold words. What a long way she had come from the Alice Spencer of topknots and prim notions. Notions. Good heavens. She had even picked up his Southern vocabulary.

Craig threw back his head and laughed. "Why, Miss Alice Spencer, I believe you are propositioning me . . . again."

"I am not," she said hotly. "You are every bit as arrogant as Lancelot. And he was positively insufferable." And how she had missed it, she thought. She hid her smile behind her menu. "I think I'll have the lamb."

"I can't abide lamb."

Craig Beaufort was determined that this would

be a proper courtship. Steeling himself against his instincts—holdovers from his wandering days—which urged him to sweep Alice off her feet and carry her, caveman-style, back to South Carolina, he showered her with orchids and candy. He was her constant companion, escorting her everywhere. Sometimes he smiled when he didn't really feel like it, and he rammed his fist into his pocket so often to keep from devouring Alice that he decided his hand was going to become permanently clenched. But still he persisted.

Alice felt like a Ping-Pong ball, bouncing between love and despair. She loved being with Craig. He was a masterful, take-charge man, equal to every situation without being obnoxious. But she hated this platonic courtship. She didn't want to be left on the doorstep with a sweet good-night kiss. She wanted to be wrapped in his arms and kissed until her eyes crossed. She wanted to feel his tongue plunder her mouth and his impatient hands inside her blouse. She wanted to be ravished.

They both became testy. They shopped together and argued about ribbons. She wanted the packages tied with red ribbons and he wanted blue. She said she had never heard of using blue at Christmastime, and he told her that she should see a Southern Christmas. At Au Beauchamp he had soft-shell crabs amandine and she had coq au vin. She said she would never eat anything still in its shell, and he said good wine should not be poured over food and wasted. They went to the movies. He wanted to see a Dirty Harry film and she wanted to see the Pink Panther. They argued over whether to hear Beethoven's Ninth performed by the Boston Pops or Verdi's *Requiem* by the Boston Symphony.

He wondered why she was not ecstatic over her proper courtship, and she wondered what had happened to her vagabond fisherman.

Two days before Christmas she marched into the kitchen and announced to Mrs. B that the courtship wasn't working.

Mrs. B turned from a tray of fruit bars she was preparing. "Give it time, Alice."

"How much time?" She sloshed coffee on her sleeve as she lifted her cup to her lips.

"Enough for both of you to know your hearts."

That was her trouble, Alice thought. She didn't know her heart. First she wanted Lance to be sensible, and then she wanted Craig to be frivolous. Lance was not Craig and Craig was not Lance, and she was going crazy trying to sort it all out. "I guess I'm confused," she admitted.

Mrs. B set the tray on the table and put her arm around Alice. "Honey, there's nothing to be confused about. Craig may wear different clothes now, but he's the same man he always was. He's warm and generous, and he loves you and Mark. That's all that matters."

"But what if this change is temporary? What if he decides that he'd rather be a vagabond after all?"

"Nothing in life is certain, Alice. You have to decide if he's worth the risk."

What Mrs. B said made sense, Alice decided. Maybe that was why Craig was keeping her at arm's length: He couldn't decide whether she was worth the risk. She sipped her coffee and attempted a carefree laugh. "I'm just being silly. Here I am prattling on about reformed vagabonds and permanent changes, and he's totally unconcerned. I'm the only one talking wedding bells. He hasn't even heard them tinkle."

"He will. Trust me." The oven timer went off and Mrs. B took out a pecan pie. "Craig's favorite. He's coming for lunch."

"Why didn't you say so?" Alice flew upstairs and jerked off her coffee-stained blouse. The doorbell was already pealing by the time she had slipped into a fluffy pink sweater and cream-colored slacks.

After lunch Craig and Alice sat in front of a fire in the den with their feet propped up on the hearth. "I think I would walk five miles for Mrs. B's pecan pie," Craig said. "It reminds me of home."

Alice was instantly alert. He had not mentioned his past since the night of his return. "Tell me about your home," she said softly.

He closed his eyes and leaned his head back against the sofa. "I can still smell Vashti's pecan pie. I would come home from school . . ." He hesitated, reluctant to dredge up the past, but knowing that he had to share this part of his life with Alice. "Vashti was the housekeeper. She always had pie or cookies set out for me in the garden room. She knew how I loved to look out over the ocean."

Alice had a vision of a little boy alone in a big house. She reached out her hand and brushed a lock of golden hair from his forehead.

He opened his eyes and smiled at her. Capturing her hand, he kissed her palm. "The garden room was one of my dreaming places."

"You never finished telling me all your dreams."

"Believe it or not, as I grew older one of my

dreams was to run the Beaufort Publishing Company. I prepared myself for that, attended the Wharton School of Business. And then . . ." He stopped and stared into the fire.

Alice scarcely breathed. Oh, Lord, she prayed, let him open up. Let him free himself from the ghost of his past just as she had freed herself of the ghost of Heather in the jungle. She squeezed his hand.

"Dad shocked us all by turning over the reins of the business as soon as I graduated. He announced that he was ready to retire and have fun. Six months later he and Mom were killed in a private plane crash on their way to Jamaica. He had deferred living until retirement and had six lousy months." Craig stopped talking as he looked backward in time, remembering the anguish, the frustration, and the determination not to repeat his dad's mistakes.

"Your parents . . . Heather," Alice said. "We are alike in many ways, aren't we, Craig?"

He pulled her into the circle of his arms, and his lips brushed her forehead. "Yes, love." They sat in silence while the fire burned low. A log cracked in the middle and sent a shower of sparks upward. Craig finally spoke. "But you stayed and I ran."

"No," she protested. Her Lancelot-Craig was too courageous to run away from anything. "You just needed time for some soul-searching."

He laughed. It was a short sound, without mirth. "It was a hell of a lot of soul-searching. Don't rationalize for me, love."

"I wasn't—"

He placed a finger over her lips. "Shh. Let me finish. I have to show you just how tarnished this knight is. I stayed with the business another year and a half after my parents died, reorganizing so that it would continue to operate in my absence. I gave my lawyer power of attorney to vote my stock, and then I disappeared into the sunset with nothing except the change in my pocket and the clothes on my back. I was obsessed with not repeating my father's mistakes."

"And you became Lancelot."

"Not right away. I wanted to forget everything about the Beauforts, so I took the name Gawain, hitchhiked to Memphis, and signed on with the *Delta Queen*. That was the first of many names and the first of many jobs. You know the rest of the story."

"Gawain. A knight of the Round Table," she said musingly. "Did you always choose a name from the legends of King Arthur?"

"Yes." He grinned at her. "Are you going to pull out your couch, Dr. Freud?"

She'd like to put him on her couch, she thought wickedly, but not to analyze his mind. "I wouldn't dream of it," she said innocently. She hoped Santa Claus didn't hear that lie. He'd probably leave a chunk of coal in her stocking.

Thinking of being on her couch made Craig's breathing a bit ragged, and he rammed his fist into his pocket so hard he nearly ripped a hole in it. He knew that another cold shower was his certain fate.

That evening, Alice just stepped from the shower when the doorbell rang. She glanced at her clock. Craig wouldn't be here for another hour. She belted her robe and sat down at her dressing table. Damn, she thought. She was getting tired of these cold showers. There was no fool like a converted virgin too long denied.

She heard footsteps downstairs as Mrs. B took care of the caller. Dreamily, she ran her brush through her hair. Sitting before the fire in the circle of Craig's arm that afternoon had been heaven. Funny. She never thought of him as Lancelot anymore. Oh, she still missed his casual attire and the way he had of appearing in the most unlikely places. But somehow Lancelot and Craig had merged, and she had fallen in love all over again.

Downstairs the doorbell sounded once more. Alice wondered what all the commotion was about.

Mrs. B stuck her head around the corner of the bedroom door. "This came for you." She handed Alice a large box.

Alice read the card. "Wear this tonight for me, love." Burning with curiosity, she opened the box. Inside lay a red velvet Victorian skating costume. She gasped with delight as she lifted it from the box. The floor-length dress had a matching cape, trimmed with ermine.

"I think I'm going to cry," she said. She had thought they were going to another Dirty Harry movie tonight.

Mrs. B wiped her brimming eyes and blew her nose. "It's the most romantic thing I've ever seen. And just wait till you see what's downstairs."

Holding the costume against her, Alice spun around the room. "There's more?" She flew down the stairs. Her breath caught in her throat when she saw her den. Orchids were everywhere. There were bouquets on the piano and the marble-topped tables. Baskets of exotic yellow and purple blossoms adorned the hearth. Delicate white moth orchids cascaded over baskets hung in the windows. Pale lavender Christmas orchids with purple throats floated in crystal brandy snifters.

Alice sat in the middle of the floor and hugged her skating costume to her chest. The intoxicating beauty filled her senses, and the man behind the dream filled her heart.

Her skates sparkled in the moonlight as she glided around Evans Pond. "I feel sixteen again," she said, and smiled up at her devastating escort. "Your skating leaves a lot to be desired, but you're by far the best-looking partner I've ever had."

Craig came to a wobbly stop. "This is your dream, love, not mine." He carefully readjusted her hood, pulling the ermine trim close around her face. "Happy?" He kissed the tip of her nose.

"Delirious." She wound her arms around his neck and kissed him on the lips. They were deliciously cold and dangerously wonderful. If she weren't careful, she thought, she'd attack him in the middle of the ice. Lord, what was taking him so long? "I'm in love with a dreammaker," she murmured against his lips.

"Make that a half-frozen dreammaker." He led her across the ice to the edge of the pond. The snow had been cleared away, and a small fire blazed beside a weathered redwood bench. Pulling her down with him, he sat on the bench within the circle of warmth emanating from the fire. "Comfortable?"

"Yes." She snuggled closer. "I could stay here forever."

He laughed. "I'm just an old Southern boy, love. Remember? The dream ends at midnight." The moonlight turned his eyes to gleaming blue crystals as he smiled at her. "Unless you're partial to frozen men."

Joy sang through her veins as she looked up at his dear face. She loved everything about him, she realized, from his golden good looks to his rich drawl. Imitating his accent, she said, "I'm *pahshul* to a man named Craig Beaufort, the man who makes dreams come true." The night wind whispered in the tree branches above their heads, and the stars beamed down in benediction. "Thank you for an unforgettable evening."

"It's my pleasure, love." He brushed his lips across her temple. "I wish I could make all your dreams come true. Now and forever."

She held her breath, waiting. A light snow had begun to fall, its varied crystals shimmering briefly on her red velvet skirt before disappearing forever. The stillness stretched between them, taut as a bowstring. Finally, Alice laughed lightly and stood up. "You can make one more dream come true. I've always wanted to solo under the stars." Her skirt billowed around her as she glided onto the ice.

Craig thought she resembled a flame as she whirled in the white wonderland of Evans Pond. He leaned back on the bench and watched her skate. The analogy seemed appropriate to him. She *was* a flame, a blaze that burned brightly in his heart. And though he longed to capture her in his arms and never let her go, he would be patient a while longer, until he was certain that together they could create a fire that would never die.

Ten

Alice couldn't remember such a wonderful Christmas. Craig had helped trim the tree on Christmas Eve and when the gifts were opened the next day he had been as excited as Mark. The house at 33 Mt. Vernon had been filled with laughter and joy and the delicious smells of roast turkey and mincemeat pie. At the day's end the four of them had popped corn on the fire and told stories until the wee hours.

She rolled over in bed and looked at the clock. Three. Would she ever sleep? She felt giddy and filled with anticipation, as if the best were yet to come.

It seemed that she had barely closed her eyes when a thunderous knocking sounded at her front door. She peered groggily at the clock. Seven A.M. Who in the world would be paying a call at seven goshawful o'clock in the morning? Holding her head to keep the room from spinning, she struggled into her robe and padded barefoot down the stairs.

"Shh. I'm coming," she whispered.

She opened the door and there was Lancelot, dressed in faded dungarees, a fisherman's knit sweater, and a down jacket. His honey-and-wheat hair was carelessly tousled, and he was grinning from ear to ear.

Her hand flew to her throat. "You're leaving." That had to be it, she thought wildly. Where was the businessman who had properly romanced her for the last few days? Where were the suit and tie? Oh, Lord, he was leaving again! She thought she might just die on the doorstep.

"Yes," he said. "I am."

"I knew you would." She could picture the head-lines: REJECTED WOMAN FOUND FROZEN.

He took her by the shoulders and guided her into the house. "We're going to freeze."

"I don't care," she said dully. "You're leaving."

"So are you."

She was so stunned by his appearance in vaga-bond attire that she didn't hear a word he said. "The tedium got to you. I knew it would."

"Hurry, my darling, and get dressed."

"Why? Do you want me to give you a farewell party?"

He kissed the tip of her nose. "No, sleepyhead. I want you to put on some warm clothes and throw a swimsuit and a change of clothes into a bag. We're heading to St. Thomas by way of Charleston."

"We? Did you say *we*?" The oxygen began to flow back to her brain.

"You adorable kook. Did you think I would leave without you?"

"But why? How? Oh, Lord, I didn't get to sleep till three o'clock this morning!"

"What you need, Miss Alice Spencer, is somebody to look after you." He put his arm around her shoulders and led her up the stairs. "Come, love. Pack that swimsuit while I write a note for Mrs. B." He swatted her on the behind and gave her a little push into her bedroom. Spotting the bed, he shook his head. "Tempting. Mighty tempting."

Alice yawned hugely and took a flight bag from the top of her closet. Still half asleep, she dressed in jeans, sweater, and wool parka. Muttering to herself, she packed her old blue swimsuit into the bag. "Good grief. I can't even swim. I must be crazy." But she was smiling all the while. Craig Beaufort was a certifiable genius, she decided. He *knew* how much she had missed her Lancelot.

He stuck his head around the corner of her room. "Ready, love?"

She grabbed her bag. "This is crazy," she said as they walked down the stairs.

"I know."

"But fun," she added as they closed the front door behind them.

"It gets better," he promised.

The taxi carried them to Logan International Airport, where Craig's private jet was waiting. He helped her aboard the ten-passenger plane and stowed her flight bag. "Do you want to sit up front in the co-pilot's seat?"

"As long as you don't ask me to fly the plane."

"The thought did cross my mind," he teased.

"My flying is comparable to my swimming."

"In that case, love, you just watch."

She did. As they ascended rapidly to thirty thousand feet, Craig explained to her that ice build-up was a problem in the winter unless they got above the clouds. She watched with fascination as the soared through the clouds. Was there nothing this man couldn't do?

"Where did you learn to fly?" she asked.

"In South Carolina. My parents gave me flying lessons as an eighteenth-birthday present. I learned on a single-engine cub and graduated to the big time three years later."

She sat in silence for a while, content to be in the clouds with Craig. If anyone had told her back in October that she would be doing such an impulsive thing, she would have been horrified. Suddenly, it occurred to her that she didn't even know where she was going, let alone when she would be back. She vaguely recalled that he had mentioned their destination, but she had been too sleepy to pay attention.

"I feel positively decadent," she said. "I don't even know where we're going."

He smiled at her. "You look positively ravishing. All dewy-eyed and fresh-faced from sleep. I may just keep you up here in the clouds forever."

"If this is a kidnapping, I highly recommend it."

"As I recall, the lady packed her own bag."

"Under duress."

He waggled his eyebrows at her. "That's a side of my personality I've been hiding from you. I'm patient to a point, and then I just take what I want."

"And?"

"I want you."

She savored his words as he explained again that they were flying to Charleston for the day and then on to St. Thomas. "It's time for you to see my ~me."

"~hat did you tell Mrs. B in the note?"

"That we were getting away for a day or two and to hold the fort until we get back."

Approximately two hours later Craig was setting the plane down in Charleston. A Beautfort Publishing Company car was waiting for them at the airport. Before Alice had time to catch her breath, Craig whisked her to the heart of town and treated her to a personal, guided tour of his office.

"It's so huge!" she exclaimed. "I never dreamed of anything so opulent. Slow down, Craig. I can't see everything with you rushing so."

"This is a whirlwind tour, love." He pulled her along the deserted hallways. Beaufort employees were still off for the holidays. "We have more important things to do."

"I'd like to know what's more important than getting to know about your work," she fumed as they got back into the car. "You know all about my work."

"You'll see." Maintaining his air of mystery, he whizzed through historic downtown Charleston and took a coastline road on the outskirts of the city.

"Don't they have speed limits here?" she asked. "Why, in Boston they'd put me in jail for driving like this."

"I'd come bail you out, darling."

That was the end of talk about driving and speed limits. When Craig said darling that way Alice melted down to the tips of her brand-new jogging shoes.

He whizzed down the virtually empty road, past squat palmetto trees to a redwood-and-glass house tucked into a secluded nook beside the ocean. Before Alice had time to catch more than a glimpse of the sprawling, modern house, he had pulled her inside.

Taking her by the hand, he raced through the house. "This is the kitchen, this is one of the downstairs baths, and the recreation room is over there." They ducked under the free-standing stairway. "Short cut," he explained. "The formal dining room, the breakfast nook, the library, and the dean are all over yonder." He gestured with his arm.

"What does 'over yonder' mean?"

"Southern lingo for close by. Come on." He practically carried her up the stairs. Pointing at various doorways, he rushed her down the hall. "Study, guest bedroom, bath, guest bedroom, nursery. And this"—he swung the door open dramatically—"is my bedroom." He gathered her into his arms. "And now that you know all there is to know about Craig Beaufort, Miss Alice Spencer, let's quit this pussyfooting around and get on with the serious business of dillydallying."

"You leave me breathless."

"Well, it's about time." Slowly, he pulled her sweater over her head and let it drop. It made a splash of blue on the cream-colored carpet. "Hmm, nice." His fingers trailed over her black silk camisole.

"It's the new me," she said breathlessly. She closed her eyes as his heated touch sent shivers down her spine.

"I approve." He eased the silk straps over her shoulders and lowered his lips to the tops of her breasts. Nudging the camisole aside, he traced a burning path across her flesh, following the line of her black lace bra.

Alice arched her neck and made a sound deep in

her throat. It had been so long, so long since she had known his touch. Her hands tangled in his hair as he unhooked her bra and caught her nipple between his teeth. Her legs went limp. With one fluid motion, he lifted her and carried her to the king-sized bed. The springs squeaked under their combined weight, and as they sank against the mattress she felt a strong sense of destiny. This was where she belonged. This was where she wanted to be. Now and forever.

Their belt buckles clashed as they embraced. "I think one of us is wearing too many clothes," Craig said.

"I think we both are." Alice sat up and unfastened his belt buckle. Marveling at his perfect form, she slid his jeans down his legs. She tossed them onto the carpet, and they landed with a dull thud. Her fingers danced in butterfly caresses on his bronzed skin. She savored the feel of him, prolonging the disrobing, letting his clothes flutter slowly to the carpet beside her silk camisole and bra.

"You're driving me wild, love." Roughly, he pulled her against his chest. "Come here." He kissed her hungrily, almost violently, until they were both gasping for breath. "I've been wanting to do that since the day I returned to Boston."

"If only you had known what I wanted to do to you!"

He smiled lazily, loving the sensual woman his Alice had become. "Why don't you show me?"

Her heart thundered in her ears as she sat up and slid her jeans down her legs. She recognized that this time would be different for them. This time they would come together with mutual love. She sensed that he knew it, too, that this would be very, very special for both of them, and that it must not be rushed.

His eyes widened as she emerged from her jeans. "White cotton panties?" A delighted grin split his face.

She nodded and spoke tartly. "*Sensible* white cotton panties. I tried the lace and silk kind. They made me itch."

He chuckled. "I never did trust a woman who wore frivolous panties."

She pulled off her panties and twirled them around her finger. A wicked gleam came into her eyes. "White cotton panties have so much more character, don't you think? Almost a mind of their own."

"Oh, I agree." He ran his fingers lightly down her smooth back. Sitting naked on his bed, teasing him, she reminded him of a wood nymph. Suddenly, she startled him with a quick motion of her hand. He roared with laughter as her panties sailed through the air and landed rakishly on the bedpost.

Smiling archly at him over her shoulder, she said, "Panties on the bedpost mean yes."

He pulled her down beside him. Still smiling, he said into her hair, "What means no?"

"Socks to bed." She shivered as his lips began to nibble her neck.

His mouth traveled slowly downward, seeking her hardened nipples. "Remind me to throw away all your socks," he said thickly. And there was no more talk as Craig Beaufort introduced himself properly to Alice Spencer.

The noonday sun was peeking through the window by the time the introduction was finished.

Alice smiled up at him. "Did anybody ever tell you that you dillydally just like Lancelot?"

"No." He kissed the tip of her nose and teased her by deliberately holding back the rest of his statement.

"Why not?" she prodded.

"Minx." He lightly pinched her bottom. "You know."

"I want to hear you say it."

He feigned a long-suffering expression. "I'm in love with a bossy woman."

"Say it." She caught his lower lip between her teeth. "Say the words or I'll eat you for lunch."

He smiled down into her eyes. "That's not such a bad idea."

"Craig!"

"All right. I give up." He held his hands up in mock surrender and slowly announced, "No, my love, for only you have dillydallied with them both."

"Ahh!" she sighed. "You know how to keep a woman happy." Although her words were lightly spoken, they were quite sincere. Lancelot-Craig had been responsible for her metamorphosis, and in a way she had been responsible for his. His love for her had transformed him from a careless vagabond into a man of purpose. But not completely, she added to herself. Today she had caught a glimpse of her beloved vagabond, and she knew that he would always be a part of the man she loved. She snuggled into his arms and contentedly closed her eyes. If she didn't catch a few more winks of sleep, she would turn into a pumpkin.

"Oh, no, you don't, sleepyhead," Craig got up and tossed her one of his robes. "I brought you here for a purpose."

"Slave driver." Yawning, she sat up. "I thought

this was the purpose." She swept her arm to encompass the wrinkled covers and the panties on the bedpost.

"Only partly." He took a gift-wrapped package from his closet shelf. "I have a belated Christmas present for you." He sat on the edge of the bed and handed the package to her. "Open it, love."

"What is it?" She shook the box. It was too heavy to be a ring, she decided. When would he talk about marriage? *Would* he talk about marriage?

"Look in the box and find out."

She had trouble with the knot, and he reached across the bed to help her. Lifting the box top, she gasped. "Our rock!" Nestled inside the paper was the rock she had threatened Craig with in the jungle. He had had it mounted against black velvet and framed inside a shadow box. Tears stung her eyes as she lifted the framed rock. "It's the most unusual gift I've ever received." She brushed aside a tear and smiled up at him. "Why did you bring it from the jungle?"

"The day after we talked about framing it, I walked back to the stream and picked it up."

"I didn't see you."

"You were asleep."

"I thought I was aware of your every movement in the Yucatán."

"You were—almost. That day you were napping inside the tent. As I recall, we had just been dilly-dallying."

She blushed. "Oh. *That* day."

"I don't know why I went back for the rock. At that time I wasn't even sure that I loved you."

She touched his golden chest through the V neck of his open robe. "Your heart knew."

He kissed her tenderly on the lips. "I'm in love with a wise woman."

She carried the rock downstairs with her, where they both prepared a huge meal. Neither of them had eaten, and it was well past noon. They ate in the breakfast nook overlooking the ocean. Alice insisted on having the rock on the table where she could look at it. It reminded her of all the things she loved about this man—his warmth, his generosity, his sense of humor, and his wonderful sentimentality. Mrs. B had been right, she decided. She just had to learn to trust. And, oh! she did trust this man. Any man who carried a sentimental rock for thousands of miles deserved trust. And much, much more.

After their meal they dressed in warm clothes and walked along the secluded beach that bordered his house on the east. Holding her hand, Craig pointed out some of the favorite haunts of his youth.

"See that sand dune? I used to sit over there and look across the ocean. Sometimes I would pretend to be a prince, defending his treasure from pirates."

"You're still a prince." She kissed him lightly on the lips, loving the salty taste of him. "I love you, Craig."

Looking down at her, his blue eyes intense, he cupped her face in his hands. "Say that again."

"I love you, Craig."

"That's the first time you've ever used my real name when you said that."

As they continued their walk she realized that she had come to love Craig, the business tycoon, just as fiercely as she had loved Lancelot, the vagabond. She felt a sense of contentment that she had never known in the jungle and on the ski slopes because now her love was reciprocated. Glancing at the sea gulls wheeling above them, she wondered when he would take that next giant step— marriage, the ultimate commitment. Soon, she hoped. But she dared not rush him. They had come so far already! She squeezed his hand. Time. He just needed more time.

They stopped beside a palmetto palm. Leaning against the tree, Craig hugged her close to his chest. "Cold?"

"This feels like heaven compared to Boston's weather."

He rested his chin atop her head and gazed out across the water. "What would you do if I . . ." He stopped.

Alice stood very still in the circle of his arms, waiting for him to continue. The gentle lap of water, the dazzling whiteness of the sea gulls, the feel of wind against her cheek—everything about this moment was indelibly etched in her mind.

"You love your job, don't you?" he asked.

"Yes."

"What would you do about your work if you were married?"

Her breath came out in a small whoosh. She hadn't realized that she had been holding it. Careful, she cautioned herself. He had not said if *we* were married.

"I would probably sell Tom a block of stock so that we would co-own the company. He's been wanting to buy in for a long time."

"But you would still want to manage it yourself." His words were a statement rather than a question. He knew that, except for Mark, Alice's work had been her whole life. He didn't want to hurt her anymore, not ever again, by asking her the wrong question. He had to be very sure.

"No," she said. "I wouldn't want to manage it myself."

He concealed the sudden rush of joy her answer gave him. "No? What would you do?"

"Tom's good. He could manage the company as well as I can. I would leave everything in his hands and go wherever my marriage took me." Like to Charleston, South Carolina, she thought. "From time to time, perhaps I would like to do a job myself. But not too often, I think." Marriage to Lancelot-Craig Beaufort would be enough for any woman.

"I see."

That was all he said. Alice tried to conceal her disappointment as they walked back to his house. The sky was beginning to pink in the west when they reached it.

"I had planned to fly to St. Thomas tonight," Craig said. "I love nighttime flying." He hung their coats in the hall closet. "But I think we'll stay here." He cocked his head, listening. "Somebody is playing my song."

"Who?"

"That rock you hung over our bed."

She wondered if "our bed" were a slip of the tongue. She hoped not. "I'll race you up the stairs," she challenged, bounding ahead of him.

"That's no fair," Craig complained when she won. "You were wearing jogging shoes." Looking down at her feet, he grinned. "*New* jogging shoes."

"I've taken up jogging to burn off some excess energy."

"I've got a better way," he said as he carried her into the bedroom and kicked the door shut.

*　　*　　*

Early the next morning they flew to St. Thomas.
Too early, Alice grumbled as she rubbed sleep from
her eyes.

"You never did tell me why we're flying to St.
Thomas."

"So that I can teach you to swim."

Only a vagabond fisherman would do such a
thing, she thought later as she leaned back and
watched the clouds float by.

They spent two glorious days in St. Thomas.
Craig helped her pick out a new swimsuit, a bright
red bikini, which he called sexy and she called
scandalous. They cavorted in the shallow water
until Alice learned to trust enough to let go. They
celebrated her first solo swim by sharing a bottle of
very potent wine. She asked why St. Thomas had
two moons, and he said that being tipsy became
her. She argued heatedly that if she were a gypsy
she would be wearing a ruby in her belly button. He
solemnly declared that an investigation was in
order. She told him later that if they kept up these
investigations, they wouldn't get back to Boston
until spring.

The days in St. Thomas were filled with love and
laughter and lighthearted companionship. But
there was no talk of separate jobs, separate cities,
and wedding bells.

Alice returned to Boston sporting a light tan and
a permanent grin. She returned alone, however.
Craig had to stay in Charleston and get back to
work. Although Alice was glad for one more indication that Craig was indeed committing himself,

giving up his vagabond lifestyle, she missed him terribly. He called every night, but still said nothing about a permanent relationship between them, nothing about marriage.

One afternoon, a week after she had returned to Boston, she was standing at her office window watching the snow fall. She felt that she would happily trade seven years of work for one hour in the arms of Craig Beaufort. If only he would give her some indication of where they were headed!

"Alice." She whirled at the sound of Tom's voice. "You wanted to see me."

"Yes," she said, sitting down behind her desk. "I want to talk to you about the Simond-Maxey account."

"The storyboards look good." He sat in the chair facing her. "You're going on location next week, aren't you?"

"No. I want you to go."

"I'm delighted, of course. But why? I thought you wanted to handle that one personally."

"I need to stay in Boston. Something"—Alice blushed in spite of herself—"might come up."

Tom grinned. "The same something that sent you flying off to St. Thomas?"

"Yes."

"I approve, Alice. I like the guy."

"Thanks, Tom. So do I."

He crossed to her desk, leaned down, and kissed her on the cheek. "Be happy. You deserve it." He straightened, grinning sheepishly. "I'd better call Kathy about this trip. She'll want to buy out every dress shop in Boston."

Alice finished her day's work, from time to time looking distractedly at the telephone. Why didn't it ring? she wondered, irritated. He had said that he would call early today. Why didn't he? Was he having an important meeting with some executive—some *female* executive? She'd pinch her ears off. Good grief, she was turning into a jealous shrew. She flung her pencil onto the desk and stomped to the window. The snow did nothing to soothe her ruffled spirits.

The sudden jangling of the phone caused her to spin around so swiftly that she banged her knee against the desk.

"Dammit," she yelled into the phone.

"What kind of greeting is that, darling?" Craig's rich Southern drawl sent familiar heat rushing through her body.

She dropped limply into her chair. "I've been expecting your call. Where are you?"

"The North Pole."

"The North Pole!"

"At least it feels like the North Pole. Why didn't you tell me January in Boston is so cold?"

"Craig! You're in Boston!"

"Yes. As matter of fact, I'm in your reception area, right outside your door."

Alice didn't wait to hear any more. She dropped the receiver and ran through her door. Catapulting herself into his arms, she covered his face with kisses. "The North Pole! You silly goose." She cupped his face with her hands. "Let me look at you. Your hair is all damp from the snow and your face looks tired and you've been working too hard and . . . Oh, Craig!" She buried her face in his neck.

"Hey, it's only been a week."

"It feels like years."

"I know, darling. For me too." He kissed her hungrily. "I've missed you, Alice. And I don't ever want to be apart from you again." His lips descended once more to capture hers in a kiss that raised the temperature in the office ten degrees.

She was breathless when they finally pulled apart. "You really know how to greet a woman," she said shakily.

"It's called Southern hospitality."

"Just don't spread it around."

"I wouldn't dream of it, love. Especially not after tonight." He reached behind him and picked up a large box. Thrusting it into her hands, he commanded, "Open it."

Alice lifted the lid and took out a hat, identical to the one she had lost on the lobster boat the day she had first met her Lancelot. A gentle smile curved her lips. He was full of sentimental surprises. "I don't wear sensible felt hats anymore, you know," she said softly.

"I know. I thought we would frame it and hang it over our bed as a reminder of the day we met."

She stood very still, gazing at her beloved Gawain-Galahad-Lancelot-Craig Beaufort. She loved him so much that her entire body sang with the knowledge. She loved the make-believe knight that he had been, and she loved the man he really was. She loved the carefree vagabond in him, and the astute businessman. She loved every golden inch of him, and if she lived to be a hundred, she knew that her love would still be as strong as it was on this day.

"*Our* bed?" she asked breathlessly.

"Yes, my darling." He kissed the tip of her nose. "For, you see, I've given up fictitious names." He kissed her forehead. "And faraway places." He kissed her cheek. "I'm looking for a permanent woman to share my bed." He kissed her lips.

"Just any woman?"

"A woman who gets tipsy on two glasses of wine and who gets hives from Dover sole. A woman who used to wear sensible felt hats and who once threatened me with a rock." He dropped on one knee and took her hand. "Will you share my bed and my life?"

She was laughing and crying all at the same time. "Is this a proposal?"

"What does it look like?"

She flung herself into his arms with such force that they tumbled onto the floor. Her arms encircled his neck and she plastered his face with kisses.

"Is that a yes?" he asked.

"What does it feel like?"

"Paradise."

Epilogue

Alice held her breath and fastened the waistband of her shorts. Looking in the mirror, she patted her rounded abdomen. In about another month she would have to get out her maternity clothes. She wondered if it would be twins again this time.

Smiling and stretching luxuriously, she walked to the window. The most marvelous thing about being pregnant, she decided, was that she could be a lazy slugabed and everybody just smiled indulgently. She looked down at the scene beside the beach. Mark, taking his role of older brother seriously, was directing the building of a sand castle. Samuel and Sarah, blond-haired miniatures of their father, squealed with all the happy abandon of five-year-olds. Mrs. B, who had been promoted to nanny, watched the proceedings from a nearby lawn chair.

Whistling snatches of "La Cucaracha," Alice tossed a pair of white cotton panties onto the bedpost and sat at her desk to catch up on her correspondence. As she perused a letter Mrs. Elisha P.

Farnsworth came in to clean the bedroom. Mrs. Farnsworth worked for the Beauforts on Tuesdays, Thursday mornings, and alternate Saturdays. She was built like a Sherman tank and had the personality of a grizzly bear. Her hair was black as a crow's wing and her face was as cold as a glacier. Everybody in the house, except Alice, was terrified of her. Craig's favorite soapbox was getting somebody less formidable to clean the house, but he never could get up the nerve to fire Mrs. Farnsworth.

While Alice worked, Mrs. Farnsworth vacuumed and dusted and scrubbed. Every so often her gaze would wander to the panties on the bedpost, and her eyebrows would shoot up into her stiffly lacquered hair. Finally she could stand it no longer. Lifting the panties, she boomed, "Shall I put these in the lingerie drawer, Mrs. Beaufort?"

"No, Farny. Leave them there." Nobody except Alice dared call her Farny.

"I see." But she didn't see at all. Mrs. Farnsworth hated mysteries, and it was a mystery to her why Mrs. Beaufort's panties were on the bedpost every Thursday. She had even discussed the matter with Effie Mae, who cleaned for the Lockridges. Effie Mae hadn't a clue, but Elizabeth, who was named for the movie star and worked Thursdays for the Scottsdales down the street, had said that she saw Mr. Beaufort's car heading home every Thursday at noon. The speculation resulting from that bit of information had elicited quite a few bawdy comments. Replacing the cotton undergarment, Mrs. Farnsworth announced, "I've finished downstairs. I'll see you next Tuesday." She was grinning as she left the room.

"Have a nice weekend, Farny," Alice called after her.

Mrs. B hustled in, leading the rosy-cheeked twins. "We came to kiss Mommy good-bye before going to the Disney matinee," she said.

Alice kissed her cherubs and spoke over the tops of their golden heads. "What about Mark?"

"He's getting his ball and bat for Little League practice. He says he's too old for that mushy stuff."

"What mushy stuff, Mommy?" Sarah asked.

"Kissin', silly," Samuel announced.

Mrs. B puffed out her chest with pride. "They're angels. Absolute angels." She took their chubby hands. "We left your lunch on the kitchen counter."

" 'Bye," Alice called. "See you at four."

She turned back to her desk and idly leafed through the storyboards Tom had sent her. She had toyed with the idea of going to Boston next week, maybe even directing the suntan oil commercial, but her heart just wasn't in it. Her whole world centered around a certain handsome publishing magnate. Hearing his car door slam, she rushed to the window. Craig was standing in the driveway with the sun glinting in his hair. Her mouth went dry.

He smiled and waved. She heard the front door close, and then his footsteps as he bounded up the stairs. She put her hand over her thundering heart. Amazing, she thought, that after all these years he could still make her shivery and weak-kneed.

He came through the bedroom door and tossed his briefcase onto a chair. Suppressing his laughter, he looked from Alice to the panties on the bedpost. He deliberately walked over to her and began to unbutton her blouse. "Darling, we're going to have to do something about this," he drawled. Her blouse fell to the floor and he reached for her shorts. "The neighbors are beginning to talk."

"What are they saying?" She unknotted his tie as her shorts slipped to the carpet.

"They're saying it's scandalous the way Mr. and Mrs. Craig Beaufort carry on." He nuzzled her neck as she finished undressing him.

"We wouldn't want to make liars of our neighbors, would we, love?" she asked, and taking his hand, led him to the bed.

"No." His voice was muffled as his mouth sought her breasts.

"So scandalize me."

And time stood still as the former Miss Alice Spencer was properly scandalized by her vagabond fisherman.

THE EDITOR'S CORNER

Ah, the crazy calendar of publishing! Here I am recovering from a far too generous Thanksgiving dinner . . . having just sent off the December 1986 LOVESWEPTs to be set into galleys . . . and preparing to tell you all about our romances for the merry month of May, although they really go on sale the first week of April. Is it any wonder that editors misdate their checks? So, as you can tell, the questionnaires we ran in our books last fall are still reaching us in large numbers as I write this. Here, then, is a quick up-date on your progress report to us about the quality of our stories. 55% of you said the quality has improved; 32% said it has remained the same; only 13% believe the quality has declined. Not bad, huh? Again, thank you so much for going through all the trouble of responding and, of course, for giving us so favorable a progress report. We'll be riding high on your faith in us, and working as hard as ever as we head into our fourth year of publishing LOVESWEPT.

Now, moving right along to those books for the merry month of May (which is really April but went to the printer last . . . oh, never mind!). Leading off our exciting quartet of love stories next month is talented Kathleen Creighton with **DELILAH'S WEAKNESS**, LOVESWEPT #139, and what a rip-roarin' good read this is! Heroine Delilah Beaumont is a spunky beauty who is trying to keep a sheep ranch going single-handedly when gorgeous Luke MacGregor crashes into her life . . . literally. Surviving her first aid, Luke decides he really wants a *slow* recuperation because Delilah's courage and loveliness have captivated him from his first sight of her. Soon, Ms. Beaumont isn't the least bit eager for him to leave either . . . but a completely unexpected link between his interests and her family's leads to surprising snafus in their courtship. A touching, humorous love story from Kathleen, who is making her debut with us. **DELILAH'S WEAK-**

(continued)

NESS is her second book. Her first, **DEMON LOVER,** came from another publisher and was very well received. We hope you'll give a big warm welcome to Kathleen as a LOVESWEPT author.

Take one winsome little boy who yearns for his big sister's happiness . . . now mix his fervent wishes with those of a great big strong handsome hunk of a doctor who's smitten with said sister . . . then add in a lovely skittish young woman whose shoulders are burdened with responsibilities . . . and you have the recipe for one of Fayrene Preston's most delicious romances ever! It's **FIRE IN THE RAIN,** LOVESWEPT #140. Emotionally wrenching and humorous by turns, **FIRE IN THE RAIN** will keep you rooting for every one of little Joey's prayers to be answered . . . while you are riveted by the wild attraction and dramatic problems that pull together and separate the beautiful Lanie and the devastatingly tender and magnetic Rand. When you've finished this romance I hope you will agree with us that it is most appropriately titled, that the sizzling love between Lanie and Rand could in fact start a **FIRE IN THE RAIN**.

We received glowing letters about Adrienne Staff's and Sally Goldenbaum's first two books, so we're sure you will be delighted to know they are back with **CRESCENDO,** LOVESWEPTS #141. In this dramatic and delightful romance the marvelous, big-hearted Ellen Farrell from **BANJO MAN** finds her true love at last—but in a man who couldn't be more different from her if he'd been born and raised on the moon! He is Armand Dante, a debonair world-famous symphony conductor . . . and target of the attentions of a score of glamorous ladies in high society as well as gossip columnists. Ellen is a simple woman and a hard working, dedicated nurse. Worlds apart, indeed, and how you'll relish the way the twains do meet in this charming tale!

And for a merry, merry May mix up (yes, I know, it's April) be sure to get **TROUBLE IN TRIPLICATE,** LOVESWEPT #142, by Barbara Boswell. The Post triplets are identical beauties and one of them has been involved with a Saxon man. When our heroine

Juliet takes up the cause of her heartbroken sister, she finds herself falling madly in love with the brother of the scoundrel who had done her triplet wrong. Hero Caine is enthralled with Juliet from the first. As the couple fights it out over their respective siblings, at last joining forces on a scheme to reunite them, they get trapped in their own romantic plot. Then, one night amid thunder storms and lightning, they discover a tempest brewing between them to rival the weather . . . and the stormy relationship of her sister and his brother. Another outrageously wonderful love story from Barbara Boswell!

Well, I may be a little confused about the calendar day, but I do know exactly what kind of day it's going to be for a romance reader like you when next month's LOVESWEPTs go on sale—a very good day for sure!

Warm regards,

Sincerely,

Carolyn Nichols

Carolyn Nichols
  Editor
LOVESWEPT
Bantam Books, Inc.
666 Fifth Avenue
New York, NY 10103

LOVESWEPT

Love Stories you'll never forget by authors you'll always remember